9.0 points

Throwing
LIKE A GIRL

WEEZIE KERR MACKEY

MARSHALL CAVENDISH

Marshall Cavendish Corporation
99 White Plains Road
Tarrytown, NY 10591
www.marshallcavendish.us

Library of Congress Cataloging-in-Publication Data
Mackey, Weezie Kerr.
Throwing like a girl / by Weezie Kerr Mackey.
p. cm.
Summary: After moving from Chicago to Dallas in the spring of her sophomore year, fifteen-year-old Ella finds that joining the softball team at her private school not only helps her make friends, it also provides unexpected opportunities to learn and grow.
ISBN 978-0-7614-5342-0
[1. Softball—Fiction. 2. Interpersonal relations—Fiction. 3. Self-actualization (Psychology)—Fiction. 4. High schools—Fiction. 5. Schools—Fiction. 6. Family life—Texas--Fiction 7. Dallas (Tex.)—Fiction.] I. Title.
PZ7.M198638Thr 2007
[Fic]—dc22
2006030233

The text of this book is set in Aldine 401.
Book design by Alex Ferrari/ferraridesign.com

Printed in China
First edition
10 9 8 7 6 5 4 3

mc Marshall Cavendish

Contents

PART I: PRESEASON . . . 7

PART II: REGULAR SEASON. . . 111

PART III: CHAMPIONSHIPS . . . 223

For Rob Mackey,
my north, my south, my east, my west

Thank you to Greenhill School in Dallas, Texas, which served unknowingly as the setting for this book. For dramatic purposes, the fictional Spring Valley Day School is not nearly as grand, warm, or spectacular a place as Greenhill. I loved working there and knowing all the great kids, amazing teachers, and generous administration.

To the extraordinary Bill Reiss, my literary agent, and Marilyn Mark, my superb editor: thank you for giving this book a chance.

To my amazing coaches, colleagues, teammates, and players: especially Lee Kennicke, Bonnie Beach, Robin Sheppard, Jo Ann De Martini, Tim Emerson, Sue Zawacki, Sarah Cigliano, Martha Brown, Laney Makin, Annie Farquhar, Lisa Lynch, Suzy Symons, Liz Valicenti, Sue Fernald, Kathryn Hamm, and Lydia Hemphill—I am forever grateful to all of you.

To Lucy Otto, Candace Martin, and Allie O'Leary for still treating me like the little sister so I don't have to look far for inspiration and for reading every version of this book and laughing in the right places. To Dawn Pratt, Heather Ford, and Nancy Mackey, for providing last-minute daycare and encouragement so late in the game.

To Anne Otto; Emmy O'Leary; Lindsay Martin; Kate, Jessie, and Lizzie Pratt; and Molly and Teri Ford. For acting as models on some days and readers on others. You're darlings.

I especially want to thank Michelle Bella, confidante and best friend in the world; my mom, Sue Felt Kerr (artist, writer, illustrator), who has read everything I've ever written about a hundred times and still gets excited about it; and my dad, Jamie Hastings Kerr, Jr., for cheering from the sidelines on and off the field.

To Conor and Matty, my shining pennies, thank you for retelling your dreams every morning and reminding me that sometimes going to the park and playing Uno is more important than anything else. And to Rob Mackey, my best pal, you delight and astonish me every day with your insights, encouragement, and good humor.

Preseason

Chapter 1

You think turning fifteen will be the best. You'll take driver's ed. You'll stop being a freshman, finally. And maybe, with the help of your three best friends, you'll learn to talk to boys better. So you spend practically the whole year happy, hopeful even, setting little goals for yourself—until your father tells you he got a promotion. Then everything changes. Then you're moving to Texas.

There's talk, for a very short time, of my mom and me staying in Chicago until I finish school. I overhear her on the phone with a friend. She's sighing a lot, laughing. She's quick to say, "Oh, we're not sure exactly. John may go down first for a while." Then a pause. "I know. It may be better for everyone if Ella finished up here. We just don't know."

A moment of indecision is always a good time to put in your two cents. I spend the next few days trying to act troubled, but thoughtful. I bring up meaningful subjects, such as world peace, summer jobs, and the Valentine's Day dance. I act as agreeable as possible to remind my parents that they'll want to do everything they can to keep me in this cheerful condition, since they already have experience with adolescence and my three older sisters.

Then one day I'm sitting on the back steps listening to my

parents in the kitchen. My father's just home from work, shaking peanuts from a jar. My mother's starting dinner. The radio's on. I'm waiting.

"I think Ella's really growing up," my mother begins.

This has real potential. There's a long pause as my father considers her position.

"What do you mean? You think she can handle the move now?"

"I do," the traitor says. "Maybe this'll give her time to adjust, and she won't spend all summer worried about the new school. She'll make friends down there. Have some fun."

"Okay, then," my father says, not needing any more persuasion.

Of course, no one asks me what I'd like to do. The decision has been made.

Before I know it, it's Valentine's Day. None of us get invited to the Hearts Afire dance, so Christine, Amy, and Jen throw a little going-away party for me at Christine's house. We have the best time listening to music, dancing, and watching movies. Her mom bakes this huge chocolate chip, heart-shaped cookie with M&M'S and butterscotch chips, and we pretty much eat the whole thing, even though we ate half the dough already. Lying on the floor, all of us feeling totally sick, my friends invent stories for me about what they think will happen in Dallas and what it'll be like at my new school. They tell me I'll suddenly be this new person, more attractive, smart, and witty, and everyone will love me, which is the hardest part to believe.

After they fall asleep I lie there with my eyes wide open, trying not to cry. The sleeping bag smells like David, Christine's older brother, and it's not a bad smell, kind of like the beach during winter. This is about as close to a boy as I've ever been, except in eighth grade when Sarah McNamara had a kissing party in her basement, and I got stuck with Jeff Melanowski, who everyone called Melon Head. We only kissed once, but it didn't really count because it was so dark and not quite on the lips.

I wonder if the boys in Texas wear cowboy hats and boots.

I'm sure I don't know how to do any of this—how to move and make new friends. How to get ready for something so foreign when everything I know and everything I remember will be in Chicago. Without me.

Chapter 2

In Dallas, everything comes across new and clean. Shiny. The neighborhoods look like suburbs instead of part of a city, like Lake View, where I used to live, where trains and buses took you anywhere you wanted to go, and the stores were only a few blocks away. Here, people drive. And everything feels far away.

Our ten-year-old house is brick with glossy black shutters and a curving front walk, edged by a weedless yard. There's no paint chipping anywhere. It's a little overconfident for my liking, with its central air and a stainless-steel refrigerator that doesn't hold magnets. My old house, on the other hand, was a rambling bungalow, and Becky and I shared a room on the third floor, which had slanted ceilings and radiators that thumped and hissed. There was something comforting about living right under the roof. Something safe.

This neighborhood is swept and mowed and clipped. "Manicured," my mother gushes.

"And the roads don't have potholes," my father adds, like we're in a commercial for how great Texas is.

I have to start my new school in two days, and each one of my older sisters calls to talk to me, which never happens. I think my parents put them up to it. Becky, who's in college in Boston, says she can't wait to come home this summer, that we can check out Dallas together. Janie ends up telling me about her new job at the ad agency since I don't say anything when she asks what's up. But Liz is pretty cool about it; she's getting married this summer so she has temporary moments of sensitivity. She says, "Are you nervous about starting your new school?"

Mom and Dad have enrolled me at Spring Valley Day School, where a coworker of my father's sends his kids.

I try to respond casually. "Not really nervous, no." Even though I am.

"What're you gonna wear the first day?"

"I'm not sure. Mom's taking me shopping."

"Don't let her talk you into something babyish."

"I won't. They actually wanted me to wear a sweatshirt they bought for me when I interviewed at the school."

"Oh, no."

"Yeah. And it's purple and green."

"Purple and green?"

"School colors."

"Oh, my."

On Monday morning, my first day, I throw up and have to change the new shirt I bought the day before. I tell my mom I decided to wear something else, and she gets mad because we took a long time at the mall to find my outfit. I can hardly talk the whole drive to school, and when we get there it's jam-packed with cars going every which way. Mom's trying not to act annoyed, but I can tell by her mouth all straight and tight that she is.

I can't see one other person my age getting dropped off by a parent. Meanwhile, we have this hideous blue station wagon that's been the family car since before I was born, practically. Each of my sisters drove it in high school, and when Becky suddenly needed a car up at college, my parents gave her the Volvo, the good car. Don't ask me why. She bugged out about it, as if they should've given her a new car or something. And now, like some bad dream, I'll be stuck with the Blue Bomber, which I swore I'd never drive in public, even with my learner's permit.

To make this moment worse, my mother actually leans over like she's planning to kiss me good-bye, and I say, "Mom," with a very firm look, so she backs off.

"Remember," she tells me, putting on a brave face, "bloom where you're planted."

Luckily no one's near enough to hear this.

I give her a weak smile, climb out of the car, and feel for the first time how out of place I am in Texas. Is it my imagination or is everyone staring at me? At my short brown, curly hair. My pale skin. My clunky, winter, midwestern shoes. My camouflage backpack, which was cool back home, now clearly stands out as some kind of fashion emergency. Most of the girls are wearing short skirts and color-coordinated sandals, with painted toenails and silver toe rings. They have highlights in their hair and complicated updos that look casual but may actually require another person to perfect. I can't believe how underdressed I am.

For a split second, I want to whip back into the car, duck down, and tell my mom to put the pedal to the metal. But I don't. I swallow the bubble in my throat and walk across the quad to the headmaster's office like I'm supposed to. His nice secretary hands me a schedule and escorts me to my first class—geometry, which is actually one of my better subjects.

The teacher, Mr. Milauskas, seems fine, geeky in that math-teacher way, but nice enough to smile when I sit down in the only open seat, smack dab in front of him, to start my new life.

The rest of the day goes along. I get introduced in every class; faces turn to stare, but that's it. Nobody leans across the aisle to make friends with me. It's March; they already have friends.

At dinner my father asks, "Did you make any new friends?"

I try not to roll my eyes. "Dad, it's my first day."

"Maybe you could join a club."

"Great idea," my mom chimes in.

Parents are so out of touch.

"It's March." I state the obvious, the same thing I've been telling myself over and over. "Everything's already decided."

"Everything?"

"It's practically summer, Dad. No one does anything now."

And *hello*, I've never in the history of my life been a club-joining type of person.

"What about a spring musical? Do they have something like that?" my mom says, as she passes me the salad.

There's really no response necessary.

Chapter 3

At my old school you just had one big four-story building. There was the principal's office, gym and auditorium, smoking area in the teachers' parking lot. Simple. The classrooms had numbers, not names, and bells rang when the period was over. The lockers lining the hallways defined you: freshmen on the fourth floor, seniors on the first, like that. You had a place in the order of things. You knew where you belonged.

But Spring Valley Day School makes me feel lost from myself. For starters, it's a campus with lots of low, modern buildings, gathered in a skinny oval: library at the top, athletic fields at the bottom, with the football stadium across the street. (The stadium has a parking lot, a snack bar, bathrooms, and lights for night games. It looks like it belongs at a college or something.) In the middle of the oval, the grassy, tree-lined quad is dissected by sidewalks that connect the separate buildings: lower, middle, and upper schools; arts and sciences; cafeteria; gyms. But the campus is top-heavy with its spectacular library, which overlooks a sweeping front lawn. When prospective parents like mine approach the campus from the long driveway, they gasp at the superior academic possibilities exhibited not only in test scores, but in the architecture as well.

THROWING LIKE A GIRL

The upper school classrooms don't have walls, just dividers, and you can hear French during Spanish and world history during geometry. The headmaster's secretary explained to me that it's a progressive way of educating, so I nodded my approval, even though it's totally distracting. Also, forget about lockers defining the internal hierarchy. Here, in the "progressive" upper school, you get cubbies painted in primary colors, like when you were in kindergarten, with all your private things on display and your lunch right out there for everyone to smell.

And then there are the peacocks, which happen to be the school mascot. Apparently the property used to be part of a peacock farm and real-live peacocks still roam the campus. The students seem to ignore them because they've been there forever. After my first few days, I'm starting to feel like a peacock myself— there, but not noticed, not yet. Which in some ways is a good thing.

By Friday, I've got a routine going. I don't ride the bus or car pool with my nonexistent friends. No, not the new girl. I still get driven by my mother, who has been instructed to wait in the drop-off lane by the lower school for "vehicle flow" purposes. At least this way the only people staring at me are less than four feet tall and I can completely ignore them. Who's the peacock now?

In P. E., my last class of the day, it's just me and a few other girls who never change clothes because they've got some medical excuse for not having to sweat off their makeup. One girl has an inner-ear imbalance and hands the coach a note. Another has her period. The others, I've no idea what their excuses are. But since they're off the hook, and the athletes at Spring Valley are exempt from P. E., I'm left with a group of boys who are in no way connected to sports or teams. And do not fit any mental image I have of boys in Texas.

They're just like boys I knew in Chicago, funny and self-conscious, smart and socially challenged, like me. We're supposed to be in week four of something called lifetime sports—things like golf and archery and tennis—but the teacher, Coach Dixon, has us playing basketball, instead. We pound up and down the court, exhausting ourselves, while Dixon calls out corrections and the girls in the bleachers look at their nails or chitchat. It makes it easier for me to participate.

Dixon blows her whistle and we break. She walks up to me. "Hey, Chicago," she says. "Where'd you learn to shoot hoops?"

I'm panting. "Uh, nowhere?"

Everyone stares at me, even the girls in the bleachers.

Coach sets up a jump ball. "You play on any team?"

I must've blushed because everyone's still looking at me, and also this is about the longest conversation I've had with anyone since I've been here.

"No." I shake my head. "I didn't play sports at my school." In a gym full of nonathletes, this makes me proud.

She tosses the ball up, and we resume play, throwing the ball back and forth, working our way downcourt, taking shots. "How come?" Dixon pushes.

"Too competitive," I huff.

She blows her whistle and doesn't say anything more.

"Watch out," one of the guys says. "She's recruiting you for the basketball team."

"Yeah, and they're not competitive at all," another one adds.

"I'm standing right here. I have ears," Dixon says.

It's still well before three, but like every day this week, she lets us go early. We all help put the basketballs back into the hopper.

Dixon says to me, "You're a good athlete, Ella. You should

look into the sports program here."

My insides sing.

As I approach the locker-room door, another coach comes out. "Hey, Dix," she says, looking up from a clipboard.

"Addie. I want you to meet a new student, Ella Kessler. Ella, this is Coach Lauer."

We shake hands.

Dixon says, "When are your softball tryouts?"

"Monday. Why?" The coach looks right at me. "Do you play?"

Before I can answer, Dixon says, "Ella just moved here from Chicago. She's a natural athlete."

"I'm new here, too," she says. "To Spring Valley. I started a month ago." She smiles. "So, if you're interested, Ella, why don't you come by the field on Monday. Three thirty. Two days of try-outs, and the team'll be posted by Wednesday. Easy as that."

"Oh, okay," I say, because she makes it sound so simple.

I change clothes in the locker room and then stand with all the second and third graders waiting for my mom to pick me up. I have no friends. No place to go this weekend. The wind is so warm and dry here, like September back home. I close my eyes to imagine Chicago right now, where it's still winter in the worst way—streets heavy with slush, the wind biting at your cheeks, your nose running, and your eyes tearing. Everyone rushes down sidewalks or stands on El platforms waiting for trains, just gazing out into the world, trying to think of anything besides the cold. I always loved winter, even when it lasted six months in Chicago.

And then some kid pokes me out of my daydream and says, "Hey, I think your ride's here."

I'm so sure.

Chapter 4

My mother asks me the same questions every day. How'd you do? How were your teachers? Are the classes too hard? Do you have a lot of homework? It makes it easy not to talk about anything important. I just answer the questions and glance in her direction every few seconds. I don't tell her about the softball thing, and how would she even know to ask?

But then, out of nowhere she says, "What else is going on? There's something, isn't there?"

We're at a stoplight. She's staring me down. It freaks me out.

"What do you mean?"

She shrugs. "I don't know. You have a look."

"A look?" I snort as I say this.

"Okay, you don't have to tell me. That's fine."

And so I keep it wrapped tight in the palm of my hand all weekend. I fix up my new room, which has a border of daisies with little flecks of yellow. Kind of babyish, but not so bad. I hook up my computer so I can start IMing Christine, Amy, and Jen and tell them how wrong they were about their predictions for me. I unpack my things and get completely organized with my classes. I spend half of a beautiful Saturday doing my homework and the other half arranging clothes in my very own closet. The house is so big I get my own bedroom, and, best of all, it's connected to my own tiny bathroom, where I can line up my lotions and shampoos on the shelf beside the tub and not have to share anything with my sisters.

Finally, on Sunday I get out and do something. My mom and I go to the library together, and while she's getting a card and looking through new fiction, I sneak to the nonfiction area and page through a book on softball.

In general, I understand the game. My dad and I watch the Cubs all summer. I know about three outs and balls and strikes. I know where each position is, and I know that a mitt is also called a glove. I haven't played since I was a kid, but I'm pretty sure I can catch and hit. Throwing might be a problem. So I find a chapter on mechanics, like catching a fly ball, fielding a grounder, swinging the bat, and pitching. Unfortunately, the section on throwing only talks about things like where to throw when you get the ball in the outfield and there's a runner on first, for example. I guess they just assume you know how to throw the ball already.

My mom rounds the corner. "There you are. I've been looking for you." She cranes her neck to see the book I'm studying. "Find something?"

I need to make a quick decision. If I shove the book back on the shelf she probably won't ask about it again and I won't have to explain that I'm trying out for a sports team. But then I won't have the book to take home with me. If I tell her I'm checking it out, she'll see it, and I'll have to tell her everything. And she'll be so excited.

I don't know which is worse.

I close the book and hold it against me. "Mom, I want to get my own library card and check out this book, but I don't want you to ask me anything about it right now. Okay?"

She opens her mouth. I can tell she has no idea what to say. She probably thinks it's a sex book or some self-help for teens on how to tell your parents you're mad they made you move someplace you never wanted to go. She glances at the other books on the shelves near me, trying to get an idea of what I'm hiding.

"Ella." She stops.

I know I should say something to help her. The truth is, what my parents said after my first day of school was right. If I joined something, a team or a club, maybe I could make some friends and have some place to go after school. I could at least go through the motions of belonging. But what if I try out for softball and don't make it? What if I'm so bad that the nice coach will take me aside on Wednesday to tell me? She'll say she really wishes there was something she could do, but I was just *so* bad. Then I'd have to come home and tell my parents, and they'd be all sorry for me. I couldn't stand that.

When I don't respond, my mother takes a deep breath. "Okay," she says finally, agreeing not to ask questions.

In the car on the way home, I tell her, "I promise to explain this at some point."

She nods without looking at me.

That night in my room with the daisies, I finish the rest of my homework and page through the softball book again, taking notes as if it's for a class. I try to picture tomorrow—going through P. E. with Dixon wishing me luck for tryouts, and the boys saying they'll miss me if I make the team. I imagine what it'll be like walking onto the softball field with all the other girls who know one another. And then I remind myself that the coach doesn't know anyone, either. This helps calm me down; it helps me fall asleep, even though I've got butterflies in my stomach.

In the morning, I carry the heavy softball book in my backpack so my mother doesn't find it in my room. During breakfast I tell her, "I'm staying after school for extra help today."

She looks all alarmed, like the school's too hard and I won't get into college.

"Don't worry," I say, but I'm pretty worried myself.

"Oh, so now I don't get to worry or ask questions or know anything about anything?" She's at the sink with her back to me.

I'm trying hard to remember if my sisters ever tortured my mother like this. Surely someone did at some point.

"Everything's fine, Mom."

The drive to school is unbearable. Now I know how she feels when I give her the silent treatment. She doesn't say a word, and I'm ready to confess everything, but I don't.

At the lower school drop-off, I make the move she tried last week: I lean over and kiss her cheek to say good-bye.

She ignores my apologetic gesture. "What time should I pick you up?"

"How about six?"

"Six! Isn't that a bit late?"

"I could call if I need you to come sooner."

She sighs. "All right." And then she looks over at me. "If there's a problem, Ella, I'd like to help."

We're holding up the car-pool line, and one of the traffic-control ladies starts waving frantically.

"It's not like that, Mom. Really, don't worry."

I get out of the car and go with the flow of lower-school kids up the sidewalk. There's a moment where I almost want to follow them inside, sit in a little chair at a little desk. But then I think about reliving junior high and my freshman year and decide against it.

Instead, I sling my 400-pound camouflage backpack over my shoulder and veer off toward the upper school—where I have to be fifteen and like it.

Chapter 5

When I was a kid, I used to take sailing lessons in the summer down at Belmont. My sisters had done it, and loved it, so then it was my turn. I spent my first year as a crew on a dinghy. All we did was tack in and around the boats anchored in the harbor. It was so safe. I learned to pull in the mainsheet and let it out. I learned to read the wind on the sail and duck my head when the boom swung from left to right. I learned to tie all the knots faster than anyone. I was good at just about everything.

Except this one thing. Kind of a big thing. I couldn't deal with the idea of going out on the lake. The harbor with its stone walls and gentle breezes was like a nest to a baby bird. But Lake Michigan, lurking beyond this peaceful shelter, was a vast, bottomless surge of waves and currents and quick storms. The thought of sailing a tiny boat out there absolutely terrified me.

My second year I graduated to skipper and learned quickly how to shout out directions to my crew, a red-haired girl from my neighborhood who was clumsy and quiet. Every morning, I'd watch the older kids sail the 420s out through the mouth of the harbor right into Lake Michigan. None of them looked nervous or sick. I could hardly stand it.

During race week I won almost every race. The older kids

learned my name and congratulated me. The teachers all had
high hopes. They told me, "Next summer you'll go out on the
lake. You'll be a real sailor."

I never went back.

When I told my mother I didn't like sailing anymore, she
said, "Do you want to try soccer camp with Christine?" She had
no clue.

I've been thinking about sailing lately. About having a fear of
something and being too afraid to face it. It's not the best way to
work something out. I know that now.

Monday drags on forever. My last class before gym is Behavioral
Science. It's my only elective and my new favorite, even though
when my father saw my schedule he said, "What happened to
chemistry and physics?" Anyway, the teacher, Mr. Dominick, is
really young and cute and talks like a teenager. The class is set up
in a big circle, a detail that makes me feel old-fashioned because
I prefer to be hidden in the middle of a row.

But today I'm distracted from the circle seating. My butterflies are back. In forty minutes I'll have P. E. and then tryouts. I'm
so nervous I hardly pay attention as Mr. Dominick explains the
project we're starting, where you get a partner and pretend you're
married.

Everyone starts laughing and my adrenaline soars because, of
course, I'm only half listening, and maybe I picked my nose by
accident?

Apparently not. Mr. Dominick goes on about the Marriage
Project; everyone will have a job, a salary, and a partner. We'll
have to figure out where we're gonna live based on how much
rent is, utilities (whatever they are), and how much gas it will take

to get to work if we have a car—and if we don't, how much it will cost to take the bus. It's pretty interesting, and everyone's talking out of turn, and he's not getting mad at us. It's kind of cool.

I pick my job out of his baseball cap: a journalist at the *Dallas Morning News*. I work for the arts section and get paid $24,000 a year. I get to go to movies for free *and* I'm rich! Next, the boys pick a girl's name, and Nate Fontineau picks me. Nate's one of the seniors in the class and everyone seems to worship him. I think he's a football player. One of his friends reads Nate's slip of paper and says, "Dude, you got the new girl." I've decided to reserve judgment until later.

I *have* noticed he tries to be really funny making jokes about his job—he's a golf pro—and I'm the only girl who doesn't laugh and fall over myself. But don't get me wrong. Nate *is* cute. He's got light brown, straight hair sweeping across his forehead and pretty blue eyes, almost like a girl's with long lashes; plus he doesn't blink a lot, as if he doesn't want to miss anything, and that's how I always feel.

Mr. Dominick tells us to rearrange ourselves and sit next to our partners. Nate doesn't get up to come to me so I stay right where I am, too.

The other girls are staring at me as if to say, *What are you, a show-off?*

Mr. Dominick saves the day. "Nate, I'm not sure you've met Ella Kessler. May I introduce you?"

"Thanks, Mr. D, but I got it." Nate gets up, casually tucks his books under his arm as if he's carrying a football over the goal line, and walks over to me. "Ella, I'm Nate, your fiancé. Is this seat taken?"

"No," I whisper, trying to be casual back to him. He's sort of being nice.

"Good. Fine. Now that everyone's settled, let's get down to business," Mr. Dominick says. "Tomorrow we'll have the wedding." Embarrassed laughter until Mr. D holds up his hand for quiet.

"Don't worry," Nate whispers. "We probably won't have to kiss at the ceremony." He smiles and looks me right in the eye.

I can't look away. I wonder if my sister Liz felt this way about Kevin, her fiancé, when she first met him.

Suddenly he says, "I was only kidding."

"I know." Too fast.

When we're left on our own to talk about the project, Nate says, "Where're you from?"

"Chicago."

"Wow. The Windy City."

I don't mention that everyone says that.

We begin filling out a questionnaire about our phony lives that has to be turned in by next Friday. Nate asks me, "Are we planning on starting a family?"

I open my mouth. Nothing.

He just laughs.

It's all so crazy. We're supposed to go to the grocery store together and pretend to buy food for a week that's within our budget. How is this gonna work? Does this mean that my mother will have to drop me off at Safeway in the Blue Bomber? Please *no*.

"You've been staring out the window ever since you started here. Are you bored, or do you hate school?"

He's noticed me. For a week. I give him a half smile.

THROWING LIKE A GIRL

He says, "Ah, she smiles," and I feel prickles all over my scalp.

"Actually I'm nervous about something."

"Aha! I'm good at nervous. What're you nervous about?"

"Trying out for softball."

"My sister plays softball," he says.

I imagine myself becoming best friends with her and sleeping over at their house.

"Did you play sports at your old school?" he asks.

"No. That's the problem."

"Well, you've got nothing to worry about. Spring Valley takes everyone. They have to. It's the passive-aggressive way of private schools. If you suck, it's up to you to quit. So they never have to deal with the parents that say, hey, you cut my kid!"

His hair falls in his face and as he jerks it out of his eyes, I get a soapy whiff of him.

I have no response.

"I'm just saying, don't be nervous. You'll make it."

"Okay. Thanks," I mutter.

Before P. E., I get my backpack out of my cubby and take a drink of water. I'm so parched I can hardly breathe without coughing.

Dixon greets me in class with a friendly swat on the back. "Nervous?" she practically screams at me.

"A little."

One of the guys in class glances at me.

"She's trying out for softball," Dixon says to him.

He offers a "Good luck," but it's kind of halfhearted, as if playing a sport makes me a traitor.

After class I'm on my own . . . which, when you think about it, is really where you are in life, even if you have a million friends and a family who loves you and a cute boyfriend and big boobs and good hair. You still have to be brave enough to do things like go out on the lake in a tiny little boat.

Now me, I'm still waiting on that one.

Chapter 6

In the locker room there's a really nice old lady who hands out towels and other equipment. Her tag reads MISS RUBY, and since this is Texas, I'm not sure if Ruby is her first or last name.

"What can I do you for?" Miss Ruby asks with a friendly twang.

"I'm trying out for softball today, but I don't have a glove."

"Oh, I don't have anything like that back here," she says. She hands me a towel and a lock. "Coach Lauer will probably be able to help you out. Don't you worry."

"Thanks," I say.

The rows of lockers are cluttered with girls changing for different sports. No one seems to be staring at me, and I'm grateful for that until I realize I don't know where I'm supposed to go next. I spot three girls with brand-new softball gloves heading out the door, so I follow them at a slight distance, silently grateful for this, too.

We walk across the entire campus—away from the track, the tennis courts, and the other fields by the parking lots. I have this sinking feeling that maybe these girls don't know where they're going, either. Maybe they're freshmen pretending to know where they are. I used to do that all the time.

When they disappear over a crest between the upper school and the library, I jog a little to catch up. And there, down the sweeping, dried-out front lawn of the school, is the softball diamond, unlined and overgrown. Off to one side sits a dilapidated set of bleachers. Steel beams and cranes are casting their shadows over the "field" from a partially constructed building just beyond it. Could this be right?

I see the coach greeting some of the girls, shaking hands. So this must be it. The softball field where all my athletic dreams will come true. It's not as scary as I expected. I'm relieved that softball seems to be the ugly stepsister sport at Spring Valley. No one will be around to see me make a fool of myself.

When Coach sees me, she raises her eyebrows. "Ella Kessler, you came. Good for you."

"Hi." I can barely look around. I feel like the shy girl at the school dance in the movies, who stands off to the side alone. The wallflower. Except there aren't any walls out here.

Coach looks at her watch, then up toward campus.

"Sue Bee, will you take a jog up to the locker room and see if you can round up any more girls? They may not know that the field has been moved down here."

Not dressed for sports, and looking slightly older than the rest of us, Sue Bee nods, tucks her clipboard under her armpit, and trots away. She's too full of purpose to be anything but the team manager.

"Well, it's three thirty," Coach says. "Why don't we start throwing around before warm-up and maybe more people will show."

One of the girls calls out, "Anne Johansson decided to run track this year."

"Okay."

"And Melanie Norman isn't trying out, either," someone else shouts.

"Thanks for the info." Coach sighs.

I wonder if any of these girls is Nate Fontineau's sister.

After everyone's paired up (and I don't have a partner), I go over to Coach, who's scribbling notes on a clipboard identical to Sue Bee's.

"I don't have a glove and—"

"Oh, right." She smiles. "I think we've got a few spares in the bag over there."

I follow her.

"Lefty or righty?"

"Lefty."

"Ooooh, I'm not sure. . . . Here we go. Great. Here's a nice worn-in one." She tosses it to me. "Ever play first base?"

"No."

"Well, let's warm up that arm and see how you look."

Everyone else is already throwing back and forth. This is the part you can't read in a book. You just have to do it. I close my eyes and quickly run through the pictures in my mind of out-fielders throwing the ball. Heaving it to the infield. I open my eyes and take a deep breath.

Coach introduces me to Frannie Howard and Maureen Bartlett. Frannie is a big girl with freckles and bushy red hair. Maureen is slight with blond bangs. I repeat this in my head, *Frannie red and Maureen bangs*, so I won't forget.

"So, you weren't on the team last year," Frannie says, but not in a mean way.

"No."

Maureen throws to me first, and the ball comes straight for

my throat. I'm so caught off guard by how fast it sails right at me, and not sure how to open my glove—pointing up or down—that I just dodge the ball altogether. Maureen yells, "Sorry!" and I run to retrieve it. I pick the ball up from the grass and realize it's bigger than I expected and not soft at all. The stitches are rough against my fingers as I stuff it into my glove.

Coach saunters over from the bleachers. "That was a tough one to gauge," she says, not just to me. She takes the ball from my hand. "Generally, all the balls below your waist, you're down, like this." She shows us with her glove, open with fingers pointing down. "If it's above the waist, you're this way." She holds her glove up. If Frannie and Maureen already know these details, they don't show it.

"Here, Ella. Throw it to me, nice and easy." Coach tosses me the ball low, and I catch it, glove down, a little puff of dust coming off the leather. I feel grit on my teeth and lick my dry lips. She takes a few steps back. "Good. Now, right back at me."

I tighten my fingers around the ball and my knuckles go white. She yells, "Loosen it up! Nice, round motion."

Nice, round motion? What does *that* mean?

I throw it, hand by my ear, and it thuds to the ground.

She picks it up and trots over. Meanwhile, Frannie, Maureen, and the six or so other girls turn to watch.

Coach puts the ball in my hand, shows me how to grip it, then stands to the side and tells me to relax my arm. "Just go limp. I'll teach you the exact motion of how to throw, and then you need to do it over and over until it's smooth and natural."

I can't do this. Not in front of everyone.

But the next thing I know, she's gently moving my hand all

the way back like I'm swimming laps in a pool. The ball is higher than my head, my elbow aligned with my shoulder.

"Weight's back on your left foot to start, since you're a lefty. Good. When you make the throw, your arm will come up higher, like this, and your weight's gonna shift to your right foot as your arm goes forward."

By now, everyone is standing in a semicircle around me as she speaks. "A lot of the power should be coming from your body, your legs. It's not about your arm as much as you think it is." She's talking to everyone now. They're all listening. "You take a step and release that ball up here, not out there."

We try it again. She adjusts my arm, my elbow, my wrist. She shows me how to take the step with my foot. And then I throw it—and it flies. The girls clap.

I can't keep my face from smiling. I have *power*.

"Not bad," Coach says. "Not bad at all." She looks at the group of us and adds, "Now you know the secret of how to throw like a *real* girl. And don't let anyone tell you that's a bad thing. Got it?"

We nod our heads obediently and go back to throwing. A few other players straggle out to the field and start to throw, too. Coach and I toss a few more together, even though it takes me about five minutes to go through my motion.

When I rejoin Frannie and Maureen, they ask me what year I am and if I've ever played before. Frannie does most of the talking. She says she and "Mo" are also in tenth grade; I make a mental note of Maureen's nickname and will remember to call myself a tenth grader from now on, since no one in Texas seems to use the word *sophomore*.

"Did you play last year?" I ask them.

"Yeah, but not in middle school," Frannie answers.

I'm less self-conscious throwing when we talk, so when Mo says, "Are you new here?" I nod my head and tell them I just moved from Chicago.

Frannie stops. "Whoa. I love Chicago. They have great improv. I want to go to Northwestern and study theater after I graduate from this fine institution."

I'm impressed. "That's cool."

"Yeah," Frannie says, smiling at me and throwing the ball.

I'm starting to get the hang of this when a car drives up a few hundred feet from us, braking hard in the rough grass. Everyone turns to look. Three girls get out and stroll over. I hear Frannie and Mo groan when they see who it is. I can feel something about to happen.

"Who's car is that?" Coach yells.

"Mine," the girl in front yells back.

"Are you here to try out for softball?"

"That's right. Are you the new coach?"

"I am." They meet in the middle, not far from where I'm throwing. "Who are you?"

"I'm Joy," the second girl says.

"I'm Gwen," says the third.

But the driver, the one with the attitude dripping off her, doesn't say anything. She squints at the coach and waits.

"What about you, what's your name?"

"Sally Fontineau."

You just *had* to know this would happen.

"Glad you could make it, Sally, but you can't park on the field."

"*This* is our field?" she says with great sarcasm.

"I know. It's not perfect."

"Our old field wasn't so hot, either," someone says.

"But at least we were next to the baseball team." Everyone laughs.

Coach gives a tight-lipped smile. "The boys' baseball team has expanded this year. They now have a varsity, JV, *and* an A squad, so they needed our diamond and dugout because it's right next to their existing field." She looks around at us. "We're here because . . . well, this was the biggest spot they had left. And won't we be center stage?" She motions to all the open space.

But, *of course*, they found room for the football field.

Coach continues, "As for the construction going on next door, it's my understanding that the board of trustees voted to sell off an unused portion of the school property to Peyton Plastics. And Peyton is building its new headquarters there."

"Yeah, and they broke ground back on the first day of school," someone adds.

We look up at the building's apparent lack of progress.

Sally says, "It doesn't take a brain surgeon to know something's afoot in Denmark."

We all stand there waiting for what's coming next. When no one says anything, Joy breaks the silence, "So, you're Coach Lauer? I'm Joy. Again. I play second base."

"Glad to have you here, Joy, but I'm not assigning positions today. Why don't you grab a ball and start throwing with Gwen?"

"And I'm supposed to . . . ?" Sally says.

"Move your car. There's a student parking lot; I'm sure you've heard about it."

"That's like ten miles away."

Coach doesn't respond. She turns toward the rest of us and

claps her hands. "Five more minutes of throwing, girls. Let's warm up those arms."

Sally finally makes it back—after we've warmed up, stretched out, introduced ourselves, and finished two drills: baserunning and fielding grounders.

The drills are fun and I blend in because everyone is making little mistakes or groaning about being rusty. I feel okay. It's not so bad here in Texas.

Coach tells Sally (without any sarcasm or meanness) to go stretch on the sidelines, and then she sends Joy off to warm up Sally's arm. When everyone's finally together, I count nineteen girls, including me. Aside from Sally, they all seem pretty friendly.

Coach passes around water bottles and then ushers us to the bleachers. "I just want to see the basics today and tomorrow. I want to see you throw, catch, and hit. You don't have to be perfect, but you have to want to play. You have to want to learn. And most important, I want you to remember that playing means being a part of this team."

I may be mistaken, but it seems like Coach looks right at Sally when she says that.

"Practice runs from three thirty to five thirty. If you're going to be late or can't make it, you need to let me know beforehand. Also, no jewelry. No tank tops. No gum. Cleats are preferred, but if you don't have any, I expect your sneakers to have laces. And for your own sake and for the sake of your feet, wear socks."

She doesn't look down at Sally's shoes, but I do. Clean, white Keds, no laces, no socks.

The coach isn't really being a hard ass. I mean, she's new. She has to set ground rules. She needs to show us where she stands, like all the teachers do on their first day. If they don't get control right away, they've lost us forever. And if you sass off like Sally Fontineau, then Coach is gonna give it right back. And you're gonna look like the loser.

Maybe this is what *I* need to do, too—set my own ground rules. Not broadcast them, but just decide them for myself. I'm almost sixteen, I should have a handle on who I am by now—right?

I see how easy it could be to slip through high school and not have to say much, not have to put yourself out there. If you don't play on a team or the chess club or write for the school paper, people might never have to notice you. But maybe that's not a good thing. Maybe you really should put yourself—your doubtful, curious, hopeful, nervous-but-willing self—out there. To see what happens.

At the end of practice we run sprints. A bunch of construction workers showed up and are sitting high along the girders of the Peyton Plastics building, watching us and cheering. No one's sure whether to laugh it off or not, but we're too busy gasping for breath to do anything about it. Coach glances up and shakes her head. I figure she'll take care of it. We walk off the field by five thirty. My first day of tryouts under my belt.

Frannie and Mo catch up to me as I'm walking back up the hill. Frannie wipes the sweat from her forehead. "My girlish figure doesn't do well in this heat," she says, and we laugh.

At the student parking lot, Mo asks, "Do you need a ride somewhere?" She jingles a set of keys. "I just got my license."

"No, thanks. I'm good," I say. "See you tomorrow." I trudge to the locker room to change clothes slowly so everyone will be gone by the time I walk down to the lower school to meet my mom. It's embarrassing, but it's my life.

In the car we hardly talk, but I see my mother take me in. My flushed cheeks and hair sweaty against my head. My hands and knees dirty. She doesn't say anything. She just drives, but she's covering up something like a smile. Like she knows.

And I guess—for once—I don't really mind.

 Chapter 7

On Tuesday we have a fire drill during Behavioral Science so I hardly even see Nate. I stare at him, though. I try not to, but I can't help it. He smiles at me once, I think—no, actually, I'm not sure. And then I realize I'm just like all those other girls who worship him. When the siren finally stops and we're allowed to return to class, Mr. Dominick tells us the wedding will be put off until tomorrow, and Nate's out of the room before I get a chance to pick up my books and catch his eye.

Am I actually disappointed the mock wedding got postponed? *Please. No.*

Today at tryouts, things seem better. Sally and the coach are ignoring each other, which works for me. I'm throwing the ball with some quiet girl, hitting my target most of the time. I stretch out, groan like everyone else because we're all sore from yesterday. During our first drill, I stand in line with Frannie and Mo as they talk about the old coach, who left to take a job in Austin, where her boyfriend lives.

I ask, "So, was she a good coach?"

"She was okay," Mo says.

"But she was tentative," Frannie adds. "Tentative doesn't work with teenagers."

Just then, I notice Dixon coming down to the field. She waves at me, and I look away as if I don't see her, even though I just had P. E. about twenty minutes ago. I feel bad, but I don't want anyone thinking I'm the coach's pet. Dixon and Coach talk by the bleachers for a little while, laughing and gesturing, until Coach calls us in for another drill.

And then it happens.

As Dixon's leaving, she yells, "Give 'em hell, Chicago!"

I look around at everyone else like I have no idea why that crazy coach would yell something like that. In totally different circumstances, I'd think it was really nice. But here, when you don't want to stand out in any way and then someone announces your presence, then it's not so nice.

Coach laughs. "She means well, Ella."

That pretty much drives the nail in the coffin. Frannie and Mo already know I'm new, but they're not the ones I'm worried about.

On cue, Sally Fontineau looks at me like I'm her new object of ridicule. "Why'd she call you that?"

I want to shrug my shoulders and pretend I have no idea. But I'd definitely get busted, so I say, "I'm from there." My voice shakes. I could die.

"You're new?" she says.

Duh, I want to shout, but of course I say nothing.

Coach jumps in. "Okay, news flash, it's still practice here." And on we go.

But something feels different. Like I'm being watched. I'm not sure I want to be noticed—not right now anyway. Not by *her*. It seems as though it should be up to me whether today I blend in with the scenery or star in the show. It's obvious that with a person like Sally Fontineau, I don't get to choose.

As I stumble around during the next drill, Kat Hunter, one of the older girls who's easily the best player on the field, comes up from behind and pats me on the back. "Good job," she says as she jogs by. For what, I'm not sure, but now she's my hero, and any time I do anything halfway decent I glance around to see if she saw it.

At the end of practice, with the construction workers up on their perches looking down at us and cheering again, Coach thanks us for working so hard during tryouts. My mind races ahead to an immediate plan of defense. Do I lag behind and run the risk of becoming Sally's target? Or do I whip off to the locker room, grab my clothes, and sneak out to the lower school?

Coach dismisses us and everyone walks toward the school in little groups. Everyone but me.

I decide to lag. Sally is far enough ahead that to come back and harass me might be too much of an effort. Plus, it looks like Frannie and Mo are waiting for me again.

"So, *Chicago*, how do you think you did?" Mo asks.

I wish she wouldn't call me that. "I don't know."

Frannie laughs. "Everyone makes the team. A few'll quit. A few'll get hurt. You'll probably be starting by the end of the season."

"She *is* a new coach and she doesn't have to pick everyone," Mo says cautiously.

"Right, but she needs at least eighteen players to scrimmage," Frannie says. "There's no point in shooting yourself in the foot. She wouldn't cut you anyway, Ella. You're good."

"Yeah," Mo agrees.

I'm completely shocked by this and can't think of anything else to say but, "I am?"

They both stare at me in disbelief.

"Yes, you are, slightly," Frannie says.

"Really, don't you know that?" Mo leans into me the way a friend does when she wants to make you feel better or trust what she's saying.

At the top of the little hill between the library and the upper school, Sally stops with her posse, Gwen and Joy, and they look down at us. Or down in the general direction of the field. I almost stop in my tracks, but I have my two foot soldiers beside me so I keep going.

On the quad, a safe distance from Sally Fontineau, Frannie says, "Don't be too worried about her."

"Who?" I'm cool as a cucumber.

Frannie grins, but doesn't say anything.

"We've known her forever," Mo adds. "Everyone feels the wrath sometime."

"But why? Why is she like that?"

As Mo pauses, Frannie says, "So you *do* know who we're talking about."

"I just don't see how she gets away with being so nasty," I say.

"She's always been popular. People let her make the rules and do whatever she wants." Mo shrugs.

We don't say anything for a minute.

"Her friends don't seem as mean," I offer.

"Gwen and Joy?" Frannie says. "Yeah, they're okay. We just try to steer clear in general."

At dinner that night my father checks in again. "So, how are you liking school?"

"Fine. It seems good."

"Any troubles with your studies?"

"No." I give my mother a look.

"And the other kids seem nice?"

"Everyone's great, Dad."

Just then, the phone rings and it's probably my sister Liz calling my mother about wedding details, and then my father won't ask any more annoying questions because we'll be alone together and it'd be too awkward.

My mom gets the phone in the kitchen. "Ell, it's for you." She's smiling ear-to-ear as she comes back into the dining room.

"Is it Christine?" I ask, leaping up.

"No, it's a boy."

A boy?

"Who?"

"I didn't ask."

My stomach flips as I take the phone and walk into the family room. "Hello?"

"Ella? It's Nate Fontineau."

Could there be any other Nate? "Oh, hi."

"I was wondering if you wanted to go to Safeway this weekend for Mr. Dominick's project, since this part is due Monday."

"Right, okay. When?"

"How about if I come pick you up on Saturday morning? Around ten?"

"Ten? That sounds good. . . ."

"You can give me directions to your house in class tomorrow, okay?"

"Sure." And then we hang up.

I sit back down at the table. My parents wait for me to say something, but I can't really breathe. How did he get my number?

I can hardly remember it myself. Why didn't he ask me in school? Is it a date? I really need to go to my room to think about this.

"May I be excused? I have so much homework tonight."

I look at my mother. I know this is killing her. Why can't I tell her that I'm anxious about softball, and a really cute boy just called so now I'm anxious about that, too?

My father breaks the silence. "Sure, honey. Go ahead."

I put my plate in the sink, and go through the family room and front hall to avoid going back through the dining room. Anything to save me from having to look my mother in the eye.

When you're fifteen and your siblings are out of the house, your parents suddenly have all this time and energy to dump on you. As if they need to overcompensate for not always having time for everyone when the house was crazy and there was a line for the bathroom and everyone was fighting over stupid stuff. Now they want to sit at dinner for hours and talk with you. They want meaningful conversations, for you to bare your soul.

Everyone always says that the youngest has it so easy. But no one ever talks about the dark side, about being the one to shoulder your parents' fears as they start to realize that once you're gone, they're on their own. Yeah. It's what I live with every day.

Chapter 8

I IM my friends in Chicago to fill them in on softball tryouts and Nate calling about going to the grocery store for the Marriage Project. No one makes a comment about softball. They only want details about *Nate the Great*. And I don't have any stories about cute things he does, only the way he looks and the way other girls treat him—is this the new shallow me?

They ask if I'm liking Texas better and I wonder myself. Because Texas is not what I thought it would be: tumbleweeds and country music, cactuses and southern accents. Sometimes I feel like I could be in any other flat state, like those in the Midwest or Florida, not that I've ever been there. Dallas is just a place with new people to meet, and many of them seem to be from other places and haven't been here very long, either.

The thing I miss the most, aside from you guys, is being able to go places without my mother driving me in the Blue Bomber, I write them. I omit the part about not having anywhere to go yet. I want them to feel sorry for me, but not *that* sorry.

In school on Wednesday, I'm dying to know if I made the team, but I wait until after third period to head down to the locker room. No one's there except a teacher I don't know. She's talking to Miss Ruby in the equipment room. I slip behind a row of lockers and pretend to be looking for something. The bulletin board is at the end of the row. I try to stand back a ways to read it but can't see the names clearly. So I take a few more steps and there it is. My name. In alphabetical order. Thirteenth name on the list. *Ella Kessler*. And Mo's name is there. And Frannie's. And Sally's. Nineteen. Everyone made it.

Okay, so maybe that's not a huge deal, but who cares? *I MADE IT!*

In Behavioral Science, Nate sits across the circle from me, as if I don't exist, until Mr. Dominick reminds us that we need to sit with our partner for the ceremony. Nate stands to come to me just as I stand to go to him. We look at each other and both start to laugh.

"You? Or me?" he says.

I just want to vault across the room, but I don't. I say, "You." Then I realize I'm not sure if that means, you come to me or I go to you.

Luckily, he nods and comes to me. "Who's wearing the pants in this family, anyway?"

And now I'm happy again, even though I think I'm getting evil glares from every girl in the class. I smile.

"Hey, guess what?" he says. "You're looking at the new Gaylord Ravenal."

I stare at him blankly.

"Gaylord Ravenal, handsome-but-troubled riverboat gambler."

"I . . . what are you . . . talking about?"

"Gaylord Ravenal. He wins the hand of the beautiful Magnolia Hawks, played by Alison Finn, by the way. It's *Show Boat*, the musical this year."

"*You're* in *Show Boat*?"

"Have you seen it before?"

"No. But I think my mother knows it by heart. I didn't know you were an actor."

"I'm not really. But I'm graduating this year. Football's over." He shrugs. "The theater teacher, Mr. Archibald, subbed in English for a few weeks last fall. He thought I had *dramatic flair. I* thought I'd try something different, you know? Everyone thinks it's crazy. What do you think, Ella Kessler?"

"Great. I think it's great."

As I look at his open, warm smile it dawns on me that he's the type of person who just has things happen for him. On a whim he tries something and, go figure, it works out. I bet all the drama kids are hating him right now.

"Hey, how'd it go with softball?" he asks.

"Just like you said. Everyone made it."

"Even Sally?"

"Yes, even Sally." Much to my surprise. Maybe Coach thinks softball will save Sally.

"She said the coach doesn't like her. But she says that about everyone."

I don't respond.

He looks at me. "What do *you* think of her? My sister?"

I've dreaded this moment and hope we can stick to the realm of softball. "She's not bad," I say. "I think she plays outfield, and we did a lot of infield drills, so she may've been a little out of her element." Uncharacteristically, the words keep coming. "Of course, I'm not a great judge since I've never played softball before."

He laughs. "I'm not asking about her athletic abilities. I already know she sucks. I'm her brother. But if she focused on it for one minute she could be a hundred times better than she is right now. No, I was asking what you think of *her*. As a person."

I pause. It's clear he cares about his sister because even though she's bad—and she really is, way worse than I am—he still thinks that if she focused, she'd be better. But even I can see it's not really about focus in her case. It's attitude. She's completely bored and lazy and irritated all the time. Still, I find it interesting that he's asking what I think of her as a person. Maybe it means he's more aware than he lets on. But does he really think I'll be honest?

Before I can answer, he says, "Remember, she's gonna be your sister-in-law. You're gonna be family."

I blush. "She's fine, Nate. I don't really know her yet."

"You think she's a spoiled brat."

Those wouldn't have been my words exactly. "No, I—"

"She is. And she can be rude and obnoxious. You should hear her at home. It drives my mom crazy. Of course, Mom drives her crazy, too." He shakes his head, laughing. "But she's all right, Ella. You'd like her if you got to know her."

I hardly think so.

And then Mr. Dominick interrupts, and it's time to exchange our wedding vows. We have to face our partners and hold hands. I could die. I'm about one inch from Nate's face, and even he seems a little embarrassed. His hands are warm. I have to look down. When I look up again everyone has their attention on Mr. Dominick, so they don't have to look into their partner's eyes and see into their souls. I turn, too, and quietly repeat the words we're supposed to say. Everyone cracks up. After the *till death do us part*, Nate squeezes my hands then lets go.

Just another day in high school.

• • •

After classes I go to the locker room as an actual member of a team for the first time. Christine, Amy, and Jen are gonna give me such a hard time and call me a jock, but they'll be proud of me, too. And they'll love the *Nate the Great* wedding update.

In the gym, stacks of boxes line the wall. A sign written in Magic Marker reads: SOFTBALL TEAM—MEET HERE FOR UNI-FORMS. And a few people are already gathered. I sit down, and one of the younger girls, a ninth grader, says, "Hi, Ella."

"Hi," I say. "Are we getting uniforms already?" It's a stupid question, but I'm trying to make up for the fact that I don't remember her name.

Her eyes widen. "Yeah. The uniforms are kind of a joke around school."

"How come?"

"You'll see."

Frannie and Mo waltz in and find a spot beside me. I'm beaming; I can't help it. I'm just so happy that someone wants to come and sit down next to me.

"Here we go," Frannie says, as Coach walks in with her clip-board.

"First, I want to congratulate everyone. I truly believed that everyone who showed up for tryouts was worthy. So, be proud of that."

We're all nodding, smiling, hip to the situation and cool with it. Except for three obvious no-shows: Gwen, Joy, and Sally.

But Coach doesn't dwell. She starts pulling out purple socks and caps from the first box. "Inside the hat is a number written in black," she says. "The stirrup socks also have a number on the inseam. Take one of each, and when I call your name tell me the number on the hat first, and then the socks. Okay? Everyone got it?"

She goes alphabetically. Kim Adams. Gwen Arden (not here yet). Maureen Bartlett (new friend). Virginia Dalmeyer. Marcie Egan (twelfth grader). Sally Fontineau (also MIA). Tammy Haljun. Karen Hernandez (the ninth grader whose name I now know and will try to use in our next chat). Frannie Howard (other new friend!). Kat Hunter (the best player). Joy Jaffee (not here, either). Holly Keith. Ella Kessler . . .

When she gets to the end, she asks us, "Anyone know where Joy and Gwen and Sally are?"

Nicki Porter, who seems to be a friend of Sally's, says, "They don't change in the locker room."

"Where do they change?"

"They think it's gross."

"Thank you, Nicki. Where do they change?"

"In the library bathroom, I think."

"Okay, moving right along. Next box." She opens it and pulls out a pair of white polyester pants with a purple and green waistband. Yikes. But not *too* bad. "Please take your size."

By four o'clock Sally and company are still not here.

"Last box has the shirts. Those of you who played last year and had a number already, please take it. Twelfth graders first."

Kat and Marcie, who were voted co-captains last year, dig through the box for their old numbers as Coach holds up one of the jerseys—purple with a small green number over the left breast—and then turns it around to show off the back. The larger number is underlined by a colorful, cursive *Lady Peacocks*.

I gasp. I don't mean to, but it's horrible. Just awful. It may as well be sequined.

52

"I had the same reaction." Coach tries to comfort me. "I asked for some new ones, but unfortunately the uniform budget went to the new baseball squad."

"What scares you more, the rainbow colors or the fact that they call us Lady Peacocks?" Frannie asks.

Mo chimes in, "Technically, we should be peahens."

"You live with it," Kat Hunter says, tugging her jersey from the box, "it makes you stronger." And we all start giggling.

I end up with number five. Frannie says she always wanted two, but it didn't exactly run in her size.

"Girls like me get numbers in the forties and fifties," she says.

Coach taps Frannie on the head with her clipboard. "Girls like you hit the ball out of the park."

It's the first time I see Frannie speechless. And maybe even blushing.

I expect Gwen, Joy, and Sally to be hanging around the field when we get down there, but they're not, and Coach doesn't mention it. We have a short practice, lots of running and hand-eye drills. She has all of us wearing our new baseball hats and I love mine. I just love it. It fits perfectly. I realize practice is fun today because I'm no longer worried about making the team. And also, of course, because Sally Fontineau is nowhere to be found.

Maybe she and Gwen and Joy have decided to quit the team. I can only hope.

Chapter 9

After I change, I rush to the lower school to wait for my mom. She's usually right on time, but if I get there a few minutes early I can pull my books out and pretend I'm studying so she won't worry about me.

Today there are two little boys waiting in my usual spot. One of them is clearly a lower schooler, but the other one looks like he could be in sixth or seventh grade. They quit fooling around when they see me coming, as if I'm a teacher or something.

I sit on the curb in front of them and get a textbook from my backpack.

The younger one says, "I'm hungry."

"Rocky'll have something in her bag for you. Don't worry."

"I'm thirsty, too."

The older one ignores this comment and looks over his shoulder. "Here she comes."

An old, dirty white station wagon with fake wood on the sides, nearly as decrepit as the Blue Bomber, rolls up. In front are two high-school girls. Even from this distance I can see they're all brothers and sisters.

I get off the curb before they run me over and step back onto the sidewalk. The girl in the passenger seat looks up for a second, then back at whatever she's reading in her lap, but I catch that she's beautiful, with dark, shiny hair and light eyes like the brothers'. The driver puts the car in park and comes around the front to help the boys in. She nods at me, and I nod back. She's wearing black jeans and red high-tops. It's a cool look.

"Rock," the little one says. "Thomas told me you might have a snack in your bag."

"I might," she says. "Put on your seat belt."

She slams the door and gives me another nod. I smile this time, because she's the big sister but she sounds like the mom, and I think that's neat since I've always wanted little brothers and sisters. Especially brothers.

From the driver's side she reaches in for her bookbag, surfaces with a few granola bars, and tosses them in the backseat. Before she gets in, she catches my eye over the top of the car. "You need a lift somewhere?"

"Me?"

"Yeah."

"Oh, no. Thanks. My mom's gonna be here any minute." I don't feel like I have to cover up the ugly truth with this girl.

She looks as if she's about to duck into the car and take off, and at that moment I have two distinct feelings. One is that I wish I could drive, too, even if the car was the Blue Bomber. The second is that I don't want her to leave.

And the funny thing is, she doesn't. She says, "I think I saw you."

"I'm sorry?" I'm not sure I heard her right.

"Playing softball. You're on the team, right?"

"Right."

"Yeah, I've seen you from the library. I have to stay late

because my sister's on the ninth grade debate team and my brothers do this after-school program. The new coach looks halfway decent."

"Uh, yeah. She seems really nice." I'm not sure where all this is going.

"The old one was pathetic. She had no concept of how to run a practice. So everyone just ignored her. When it came to a game, she didn't know how to judge the other team's strengths and translate that into our game, you know what I'm saying? Basically, she couldn't coach."

Who is this girl?

I glance down at the sister who is shaking her head slightly. Rocky sees this and adds, "Theresa hates when I talk about softball."

"Did you play on the team?"

Her pale green eyes flicker. She looks beyond me. "I did. In eighth and ninth grade."

"Did you not like it?"

"No, it just cut into my schedule. I needed to change my priorities. You have to have your priorities, right?"

"Right."

"Rocky," one of the little brothers calls.

"I should go," she says. "I'm Rocky O'Hara, by the way."

"Ella Kessler."

"Okay, well, good luck this season. And keep working on that arm, Ella. It's getting better." She climbs into the car, and they rumble out of the parking lot.

I'm slightly annoyed by that arm comment, but curious, too, in a way. She sounds like she might know about softball. But she stopped playing in ninth grade. How good could she be?

My mom drives up and has to lean over to unlock my door because the Blue Bomber is so old it still has manual locks.

"Hi," I say in a sing-songy voice. I shove my bag on the floor and say it before she can: "How was your day, Mom?"

"Fine. How was yours?" She's looking amused, with a half smile.

"Good, really good." I smile at her, and her face lights up. It's amazing how easy it is to make my mother happy. "Can we stop somewhere on the way home?"

"What did you have in mind?" my mother asks playfully.

"Sport Town. I need to buy a softball glove and some cleats."

I don't know what I expected. Maybe I thought she'd pull over and hug me or let out some wild, whooping laugh, then ask a million questions. But all she does is grin. "Sure, sweetheart. I think there's one near the mall."

And for some crazy reason, that makes me extra happy. Probably because it means she knows me well enough to know I'm relieved to spill my secret at last, but I'll talk about the details later. On occasion, moms can really get you.

Chapter 10

The cute check-out guy at Sport Town says something that makes me reconsider his looks and his brain. "This is a lefty glove," he says, before scanning the price tag. "Which means it goes on your *right* hand, not your left."

I give my mother an *Is-this-guy-for-real* look.

"You still want it?" This question he directs to my mother.

She takes a deep breath. "If it were up to me, I'd say no, and then I'd ask to see your supervisor to tell him why the store has lost a customer. But it's not up to me. It's up to my daughter. The *lefty*."

I can't think of anything better to say.

"Yes," my mother says annoyed. "We'll take it."

The guy has no idea what's taken place. Or how close he came to seeing the full fury of an insulted mother defending her daughter.

In the parking lot she's still fuming. "Don't marry that boy, Ella," she blurts.

I burst out laughing. "Mom, he's, like, twenty."

At dinner I tell my parents the details of tryouts, except the part about everyone making it. And then my mother completely embellishes the Sport Town episode. My dad's cracking up so hard he has to push his chair out and lean over to catch his breath. It's pretty funny. We sit at the table forever until my mother notices it's almost nine and says, "Lord, Ella, it's late. You've got homework and practice tomorrow. I want you in bed before eleven, young lady."

I can tell things are about to change around here. And I think I'm gonna like it.

I see Nate in the cafeteria the next day. I've started sitting with Frannie and Mo (although today I'm also looking around for Rocky O'Hara), and when I get up to clear my tray, he comes over from his table of cool sports guys.

"Hey, I forgot to get directions to your house yesterday in class." He has a notebook open and a pen poised.

I give him my address and the general area where I live. I still don't know the exact street names.

"Right, I'll find it."

When we get out on the quad, Frannie and Mo give me the eye. "What was that all about?" Frannie asks, point blank.

"What?"

"Do you know who that is?" Mo asks.

"I know he's Sally's brother, if that's what you mean. He's in my Behavioral Science class. We're just partners on this project."

"The Marriage Project?" Mo asks, eyes wide.

"Yeah, did you take that class, too?"

"*Everyone* knows about the Marriage Project," Frannie says. "You can't believe the drama. Real-life couples breaking up. Jealous boyfriends. It's insane. I've never taken the class personally."

I think of the evil eyes I receive daily and start to get the picture.

"I think he likes you," Mo says.

"He's only, like, jumping up from the jock shop to talk to you," Frannie adds. "It's Sandy and Danny Zuko all over again."

When I look clueless, she says, "Don't tell me you've never seen *Grease*."

"Oh, right, that movie my parents loved a million years ago?"

Frannie smirks.

"We're just going to Safeway on Saturday—that's it!"

Frannie gives Mo a knowing look. "It always starts at the Safeway."

Chapter 11

Mr. Dominick breaks up the couples, girls in one corner, boys in the corner farthest from us. I don't even look for Nate. We drag our chairs to our respective spots. As everyone settles in new seats, Mr. Dominick explains that we'll be giving little progress reports on what we've accomplished so far, and that the others in the group may feel free to comment. He stresses that this is very informal. But still, I immediately feel sick.

The girls all seem to be sitting with their friends, and I keep trying to remind myself that I haven't even been here two weeks. I can't expect people to treat me like a best friend. I take a deep breath and open my spiral notebook. Someone is already talking. She says, "Chris and I are *so* getting divorced. I can feel it."

Everyone laughs. I laugh, too.

"He wants me to do everything related to the house," she continues, "which is everything Mr. Dominick has assigned us: groceries, budgets, finding a place to live. I mean, *please*. I'm the surgeon. He's only a struggling actor. I think he can fit in a few things between his auditions. We just yell at each other on the phone. He wants to live in a condo with a swimming pool." She rolls her eyes.

"So does Mike," another girl says; I think her name is Alicia.

"Kevin wants to live on a golf course and buy a flat-screen TV," says another.

It goes around like this. When it's my turn I feel my face get hot. "Nate and I prepared a budget based on our salaries, and we're going to Safeway on Saturday to figure out what we can afford to eat each week. That's as far as we've gotten."

I look up and bite the inside of my cheek. Should I have made it seem like we don't get along and everything he does bothers me?

There's a long, and what I would call uncomfortable, silence.

"Are you meeting there?" Alicia asks.

"What?"

"At Safeway."

"He's picking me up."

Alicia looks alarmed.

"At your house?" another girl asks.

I nod.

A few girls look at each other like they're completely confused. Another girl scribbles something on her spiral notebook and subtly pushes it to her neighbor. Two others scoff and laugh. And then it's someone else's turn. No one looks at me anymore. Thank God.

After class I want to disappear, but Nate comes up to me. "Did you say nice things about me?" he asks as we walk out of the room together.

"I . . . I didn't say much," I stammer. "I talked about our budget and getting groceries. That's it."

He stops as we step out into the hallway. "What's the matter?"

I can't look him in the eye. I know it sounds stupid, but I think I'm about to cry.

"Ella," he says. "What's wrong?"

Even though I'm feeling massively confused, I'm able to

manage a clear thought: "Every girl in this class hates me because I got you as my partner, and because you're actually doing the work, and we're going grocery shopping together, and you're picking me up at my house. . . ." I'm seriously on the verge of crying. It's completely embarrassing.

When I finally look at him, his mouth is open as if he's going to say something, but he waits, his eyes warm and patient.

"All the other husbands are losers," I blurt out.

This makes him laugh, chin lifted and eyes closed. After a moment he says, "Ella, don't worry about them. Let's go do our thing on Saturday and ace this project, okay? Ten o'clock?"

"Right," I say, but does acing this project mean ruining my chances of ever having friends here?

In the library, my hideout before practice, I look for Rocky near the windows facing the softball field, but I can't find her, so I wander down to the desks by the stacks and unload my American History book. After a few minutes I hear voices. Girls. I hold my breath and don't turn a page, hoping no one will discover me and my peaceful study spot. But they do. Sally Fontineau and Gwen and Joy: the holy trinity. I try to act casual as they come toward me like Charlie's Angels with their lip gloss and pretty hair.

"*Chicago*, I wanted to let you know that you'll have to change jerseys," Sally says, snotty and bored at the same time.

I look at her blankly.

"The softball number you picked yesterday? Five? It's taken. That was my number last year."

"Oh . . ."

"Joy is three, Gwen's four, I'm five." She shrugs. "That's not too complicated, for you, is it?"

There's a pit in my stomach that I always feel when I'm nervous. It prevents me from being able to say anything remotely coherent, as if my brain freezes up. I have it now, that feeling. I'm incapable of arguing with Sally Fontineau.

"Fine. Whatever," I end up saying.

She doesn't raise an eyebrow, doesn't even look disgusted at my inability to defend myself. She just smiles as if this was easier than she thought.

"I've already told Miss Ruby you're coming in. You should probably exchange it before practice because you don't want to be late, right? Don't want to disappoint the new coach."

I guess this is my cue, but I don't move. A few seconds go by. She levels me with her evil eye, and I *cannot believe* Nate is related to her.

And then, out of nowhere, Rocky appears from behind me. Sally looks up startled for a second then says, "Hey," all cool.

Rocky doesn't acknowledge Sally or Joy or Gwen. She taps me on the shoulder and says, "Hi, Ella."

I turn and say, "Hi," but I don't quite have my voice yet.

"Are you getting any studying done?"

I don't say anything. I can see this really isn't about me.

Joy and Gwen are already walking away when Sally throws out her parting words, "So anyway, don't forget to see the Rubes before practice, *Chicago*." She points at Rocky. "Don't be a stranger." Then she turns and leaves.

After they're gone I let out a sigh and say, "What's up?" as if my whole life is no big deal and I'm just coasting along.

Rocky laughs at me, which I appreciate, but not that much.

"Don't let her get a hold on you, Ella. She's not mean on purpose. She can't help it. She's got her own set of problems going on at home."

I don't ask details because whatever it is, it hasn't affected Nate.

"Anyway, I've been thinking maybe I could drive you home after practice, like a car pool. You get out at the same time we do. It'd save your mom a trip. You could tell me about softball."

"Wow. Really? That's so nice."

She shrugs. "Yeah. Well, think about it and see what your mom says."

"I will. Thanks." I start to shove my books into my backpack.

"You heading off to practice now?"

It sounds like she misses it. "Yeah. But I need to go change my uniform with Miss Ruby first."

"Is that what it was all about? With Sally? She's making you change your number?"

"She's not *making* me," I say. After a minute I add, "They've got some number sequence thing going, and it was her number last year."

"Look, I saw them yesterday, Ella. I saw them waiting for the team for a half hour. Obviously they skipped the part where Coach hands out the uniforms. That's not your fault. You shouldn't have to change your jersey."

"Well, at this point what am I supposed to do?"

She's quiet.

"It's not worth it," I add.

She nods. "Okay. I get that."

"Don't worry about me."

She laughs. "I'll remember that next time the Terrorizer Bunny comes down to visit you in the stacks."

I roll my eyes.

"I meant what I said. She's got nothing on you. And you're a much better softball player, anyway. Trust me."

"Thanks," I say. "And you're sure it's okay about the carpooling?

I live past the mall. Plus, your sister. She won't mind?"

"Theresa? She'll be fine."

In the locker room I go up to Miss Ruby's window and begin to explain about the jersey, trying to be as vague as possible. She nods, turns, and hands me another one. "Will this do?" she asks, giving me a wink.

I unfold it to check the size, and the number jumps out at me: SIX.

"Uhhh. . . ," I say.

I can't be six with three, four, and five taken by Sally and her thugs.

"I don't think . . ."

"Oh, darlin', this is the perfect response to the whole ball of wax. You have to take some kind of stance."

Even the equipment room lady has an opinion. And more courage than me apparently.

She looks at me for a minute, then says, "I have a few more numbers for you in case you change your mind. But why don't you think on it a while and let me know?"

I look Miss Ruby in the eye. She has a really pretty, round face, and even though her eyes sink into her wrinkly folds of skin, they shine when she smiles.

"Thank you, Miss Ruby," I say, shoving the number six jersey into my bag.

"You're welcome, Miss Ella," she says right back.

Chapter 12

I hit the field with Frannie and Mo just before three thirty. We see the coach stomping around, picking up debris all over the field.

Frannie says, "Coach, what is this stuff?"

"Construction workers," she mutters.

"They're throwing trash on the field?" Mo asks.

"Not exactly." Coach sighs. "But it's from the construction site, this material or scrap or crap, whatever you call it. I'm surprised I haven't found any nails or shards of glass."

"Well, at least we know they're eating well," Frannie says, raising a handful of fast-food cups and wrappers.

Everyone who is here (and it's just about everyone, except Sally, Gwen, and Joy—big surprise there) starts to help pick up.

"Every day I get here early and clean this field," Coach says. "Every day I tell my boss we need to talk to someone over there. Every day—nothing." She dumps an armload of junk into the garbage can by the bleachers.

"Why don't you go over and say something yourself?" Marcie suggests.

"Why don't we stretch out and start throwing," she says back.

So we do. In the middle of stretching, Sally arrives. I completely ignore her. As we start throwing back and forth, I look at the library, and almost wave to Rocky, who might be watching.

Coach, in the meantime, is looking up at the girders along the Peyton Plastics building, where our construction workers will gather after four.

Suddenly she says to us, "Fine. I'll talk to someone. I'll go after practice today."

I glance at Sally. She has no idea what Coach is talking about, and I feel a certain satisfaction in this.

"Why not go now?" Frannie says, happy to instigate. "Take us with you."

Coach opens her mouth.

"Safety in numbers, right?" Frannie says before Coach can utter a word.

Coach looks around at all of us. "All right. We go over, demand to talk to someone and,"—she glances at her watch—"get back here in ten minutes. Anyone not okay with that?"

When one girl raises her hand, everyone near her slaps it down and tells her to live a little. And that's that.

In a clump, we do a team run down the school drive to the main road and take a right. We jog inside a row of orange cones and construction vehicles.

Sally's near the back, but I can still hear her panting, "Where-the-hell-are-we-going?"

"Stay inside the cones," Coach yells back to us. We follow her through an opening in the fence and slow to a walk as a group of construction workers notices us and one steps forward.

"Can I help you ladies?" He's got a big old grin on his face and a belly to match.

"I need to talk to someone in charge about a litter problem created by Peyton Plastics, carried out by your construction company, and inflicted upon the Spring Valley campus. Can you help me with that?"

His smile fades, along with the brightness in his eyes. "Right over there." He points to a white trailer with ALCHEMY CONSTRUCTION written on the side. "You go on in, and tell Gloria about your complaint."

We move like a huge blob to the trailer. It's strangely exciting to be protesters.

Inside, it's tight with all of us standing there. Coach pushes up to the front and I can't even see the lady called Gloria, but she's got a thick accent. "Good Lord in heaven," she says, laughing. "I'll be right with you ladies."

She says good-bye to whoever she's talking to and hangs up the phone. "Now, how can I help you?"

"I need to meet with the person who runs this job site," Coach says.

Oh, that was good. Forceful.

"That would be Mr. Elliot. Let me look at his calendar."

"This won't take long at all. I guarantee."

"And your name?"

"Addie. Lauer. I'm the softball coach at Spring Valley, and we have a bit of a trash problem on our field."

"Oh, you're the gals playing right in our armpit, aren't you?"

"That's one way of putting it."

"And you say you've got trash on the field?"

"Every day. And every day I pick it up, and it's getting worse. Not to mention there would be a great liability for Peyton Plastics and Alchemy Construction if any of my girls were to get hurt by some stray piece of debris."

"Or a flying McFlurry cup," Frannie says, always the comic relief.

Gloria takes this in stride. "Let me see if I can get ahold of Mr. Elliot for you."

The tiny trailer full of girls is silent as Gloria picks up the phone. And just as she does, the door beside me opens and this totally gorgeous construction guy walks in. He's dirty and sunburned and completely undaunted by the gaggle of girls, obviously amused by the chaos. He calls out, "Gloria, are you in here somewhere?"

Everyone laughs.

"I'm here, clinging to my desk," she says. And we laugh again, though I'm not sure how Coach is taking it. "I'm trying to arrange a meeting with Mr. Elliot for some time today. It's a problem with the Spring Valley softball coach."

"Not the coach, the field," Coach corrects quickly. "Our field is getting trashed by your company."

The cute construction guy works his way to the front of the crowd. There's a perfect opening for me to see Coach's face when he says, "I can help with that. I'll take care of it."

She doesn't flinch, not even when he smiles, not even when he takes off his hard hat and reveals this beautiful head of black curly hair.

"Look, that's really sweet of you," she says, "but I want to meet with the person in charge. Our athletic director has called every day this week and gotten no response from anyone. I want this Mr. Elliot to come down to our field and see the stuff I throw into our garbage every day."

"I can arrange that." He's so calm.

"Today?"

"Yes. Today."

Gloria jumps in. "He'll come to the field in the next hour. You've got my word on it."

"Okay, then. Thank you." Coach turns, but we're all watching the action so intently that she can't budge, and her great exit is foiled by the very people who convinced her to come in the first place. She leans, bites her lip. "Ella, is that you? Could you get everything moving here?"

Someone shoves me toward the door, and I struggle to push it open. I'm yanking and whirling the little door handle. I can feel everyone's impatience and embarrassment at my inability to open it.

"Just turn it to the right, honey," Gloria calls. "And then *pull* it."

Pull. Thanks. Got it.

Back on the field, we're chatty and laughing but Coach is all biz. "Okay, let's sit on the bleachers and have a quick talk about tomorrow, next week's practices, and our first game, which is a week from today."

We climb onto the bleachers.

"By the way, I think that protest went really well, Coach," someone says.

"Yeah, especially with the cute guy in the trailer," another adds.

"Right. Mr. I-can-take-care-of-that."

"Okay, okay. Enough," Coach says. "And no foolin' around when Mr. Elliot comes by. I want this situation to get better, not worse."

We calm down a little, and she starts to talk about creating a lineup tonight, scrimmaging tomorrow, and working through our strategies next week. I feel a little buzz of adrenaline when she mentions the first game. She has schedules for us to pick up at the end of practice and asks us please to make sure we let her know if we have any conflicts throughout the season. Just as she's about to explain our first drill, some guy crosses onto the grass from the school driveway. He's in jeans, no hard hat, and as he gets closer, I can see that he looks remarkably similar to the guy in the trailer. The whole team is watching, except Coach, who has her back to him.

Finally she says, "Hello, is anyone listening to me?"

Mo points. I'm pretty sure we all know he *is* the same guy from the trailer.

He seems to be frowning a little when Coach turns, like he's not sure how she's gonna react.

"Oh, what, Mr. Elliot couldn't make it?"

"Not exactly."

Coach stands there with her hands on her hips.

"I'm . . . Mr. Elliot. Mack, actually. Mack Elliot." He extends his hand. "And I want to apologize for the trash problem—"

"*You* are Mr. Elliot? You're the one in charge?"

"I'm sorry."

"Sorry? You and Gloria were playing a little trick on me."

"It wasn't intentional. It kind of evolved."

"Evolved?"

I hate how she keeps repeating everything he says.

"Please." His voice sounds really sincere. "Accept my apology for that, too."

Coach looks down. We're so quiet that she has to glance back at us, to check if we're still there.

Personally, I think it's kind of romantic.

"Umm . . ." She laughs and shakes her head. "I'm not sure what to think," she begins. "I'm a little humiliated in front of my team, that's for sure. What does this mean about my field getting cleaned?" She looks up at him. "Was that a hoax, too?"

"No. You have my word. It'll be taken care of."

"Your word? Great. I'll be holding my breath. And there's another thing." She points to the girder eight floors up. "Those guys." About ten workers hoist their hard hats at us.

We start waving.

"Stop that," Coach scolds.

"Don't worry," Mack says. "I'll take care of that, too."

"But . . ." Debra Lester, a tenth grader, stands up. "We like that we have fans," she says.

"Yeah," a couple of other voices chime in.

Coach is fed up. "Okay, cancel that," she says with a sigh. "Just the trash."

"No problem," he says.

Sensing his departure, we start clapping. I don't know who started it, probably Frannie, but he stops to turn and bow and then he grins so wickedly behind Coach's back that we laugh and hoot and whistle until she holds up her clipboard to signal it's time to get on with practice. After all, our fans are here watching.

That night, after dinner, I help with the dishes. My father fiddles with an old camera at the kitchen table while my mother stares at me suspiciously.

"What's that look for?" I ask.

She smiles. "You haven't done dishes since softball started. That's all."

"I would. But you told me since I had practice every day that I could go straight to my room for homework."

She nods.

"By the way, I met this girl at school. She's a year older and she has her license. Her name is Rocky."

"Rocky?"

"She offered to drive me home after practice. She's in charge of her sister and brothers. Rocky has to drive them, too."

"She doesn't mind adding you to the pack?" My mother glances at my father.

"She didn't say it was a problem."

"This girl's doing this out of the goodness of her heart?" my father asks. "Out of left field, as it were?" He chuckles at his pun.

"Dad." I glance at him impatiently. "She wants to talk about softball. She used to play, but there's too much else going on at home now."

There is some kind of over-my-shoulder secret nod of approval between my parents.

"Okay," my mom says. Simple as that.

Chapter 13

By lunch on Friday, Frannie, Mo, and I are unanimous that Coach and Mack Elliot would be a perfect couple, even though we know next to nothing about either of them.

"He's just the right height," Mo says.

"He's got the best name, too. And that curly hair." Frannie sighs.

"And good hands," I add.

"Like yours when you were trying to open the trailer door," Frannie says.

When I reenact my door-opening mishap for the third time, we laugh so hard we almost choke on our tuna melts.

"It was one of those where you can't tell if it swings in or out," I say in my defense, making them laugh more.

"What if she already has a boyfriend?" Mo interrupts earnestly.

"What if *so what*?" Frannie says. "He has charisma. You can tell."

"She didn't seem too happy about the practical joke," I note.

"No," Mo agrees, shaking her head.

"Come on, they'll laugh about it one day. Y'all are such worrywarts," Frannie says.

"Speaking of which, are you worried about the lineup Coach is working on?" I ask.

They look at me as if I'm crazy.

"Ella, it's not gonna affect us," Mo says.

My heart sinks. "You mean because we won't be starting?"

"*You* might be." Mo always wants to say encouraging things.

"It's only the first game, Ella," Frannie says. "And we're not exactly Rocky O'Haras."

I look at her. "How do you know about her?"

"How do *you*?" she fires back.

"Well, I know she used to play."

"Yeah, she used to play. She used to be the best player we ever had," Frannie says.

"Then why isn't she on the team anymore?"

Frannie and Mo exchange looks. I raise my eyebrows to alert them that I'm ready for the long story.

"It's sort of because her mom died," Mo says. "That was seventh grade. Her aunt helped her dad out, but then the aunt had her own family to take care of."

"How'd she die?" I whisper.

"Cancer," Mo whispers back. And then in her normal voice, "So, that year she came to school, but she didn't play any sports. In eighth grade, though, she tried out and was so good they put her on varsity, which is unheard of, you know. And then again in ninth grade. But by the spring of tenth grade—that was last year—Rocky got her license, and that was the end of her softball career. The aunt went back to her life, and Rocky gave up her own."

"Which was especially unfair because she has this older brother," Frannie says, "who graduated last year."

"Why doesn't he help out?" I ask.

"Anthony is a phenomenal football player," Frannie explains. "Spring Valley recruited him when he was in eighth grade. They got all the kids, the whole family, into the school on scholarships because of him. Nobody was going to ask *him* to quit football or rearrange his schedule."

"So, how do *you* know about her?" Mo asks, and I must have a blank look on my face because she asks again.

"Oh, I met her over by the lower school."

"You met Rocky?" As if she's some sort of celebrity.

"She picks up her sister and brothers at the same time my mom picks me up. She told me she watches practice from the library while she waits to drive everybody home."

"She watches practice from the libes?" Frannie asks.

"That's kind of sad," Mo says.

"What's sad is her brother," Frannie counters. "He's the cutest guy. The best football player we'd had in years. College scouts came to see him play. And then he blew out his knee at homecoming. Supposedly a doctor told him he'd never play football again. So, he didn't go to college. He got a job with Mr. O'Hara, who's a security guard in some fancy hotel downtown. And that's it. He still lives at home. He still doesn't help out Rocky. Nothing. She's stuck."

I just sit there and try to take it in. I can't finish my yogurt. I can't even look at my chocolate chip cookie.

And then Rocky appears at our table. It's shocking really. We're stunned into silence.

"Hey," she says to us, then to me, "Did you talk to your mom?"

"Yeah. She's thrilled she doesn't have to pick me up anymore."

Rocky smiles. "Good. I'll see you around five forty-five?"

"Sure."

"Bye." Rocky nods.

Mo says, "She's so nice."

"Totally," Frannie adds.

I'm excited and nervous about softball the whole day. During Behavioral Science someone tells Mr. Dominick that Nate is absent today, and I'd been so distracted by softball I hardly even noticed!

I realize that reading a lineup (with only nine players) and scrimmaging isn't a huge deal, but it's the first time I've ever played a real game, and I want to be good. I want to understand every position and where you're supposed to be on the field. I want to be able to read a batter, which is something Coach mentioned yesterday, and people nodded their heads, and I had no idea what she was talking about. I need to remember to look that up online tonight.

Mostly, I want to hit the ball and get on base. I want to learn to slide. I want to cross home plate and have the whole team high-five me. And I want to throw like a girl. A *real* girl.

Chapter 14

Coach reads two lineups. The *good* lineup is on the field, and Coach is barking instructions at them. They seem pumped and confident. The rest of us kick around in the dirt, waiting to hear what we're supposed to do and gazing at the bats leaning against the fence.

"Okay," Coach says when she finally comes over to us, the leftovers. "Y'all are up. Everyone will bat. And then we'll put you out in the field for one rotation. To make things go a little faster, each batter gets three pitches. Kat's catching; she'll make the calls. If the three pitches are balls, then you walk. But if one's good, you swing away. I'll be coaching from first. We won't work on signs or anything today. Just hit the ball."

I swear she's talking so fast I hardly understand anything she says. And worse than that, Sally Fontineau is also on the bad squad, or as Frannie has nicknamed us already, the Bod Squad.

I'm up third. LeaAnne LaRusso (a ninth grader) explains to me that it's because I'm playing first base and we're going in order of positions—pitcher, catcher, first—not ability.

"Thanks, LeaAnne," I say, trying not to sound sarcastic.

Gwen Arden, Sally's gal pal, is pitching. She's pretty good

actually, and after two foul tips, she strikes out Jenny Yin, and everyone on the field cheers.

This sucks.

LeaAnne catches for our team, so she's up next. She's pretty good. If Kat weren't the best player on the team, LeaAnne might have a shot at starting catcher. But what do I know?

She swings at the first pitch. I'm watching her feet dig a place for themselves at the plate. She holds her right elbow up high, and even though her stance looks funny, she hits it over Virginia Dalmeyer's head. It's not a really hard hit, but it gets her to first. Virginia's playing short but, according to Frannie, that was Rocky's position and Virginia's better at third.

Anyway, blah blah. I'm up next and everyone's watching me. Why did I want to play this stupid sport? It's supposedly a team sport, but really it's one more opportunity for everyone to stare at the new girl from Chicago who has never played softball before. *Totally humiliating.*

I try to remember what LeaAnne did. Since I'm a lefty, I have to do everything opposite, but I manage to do it. I stand there trying to stare down Gwen, when LeaAnne yells, "Come on, Ella!"

It's as if the sky opened up and the gods shoved a big old spike of adrenaline into my heart. I have to scowl on purpose so I don't smile. I want to yell thank you to LeaAnne, but suddenly the first pitch goes flying past me and slams into Kat's glove.

Kat rises from her squat and tosses the ball back to Gwen so effortlessly that I have to look at her. She grins through her catcher's mask. "Nice and easy, Ella," she says. "Don't take your eye off that ball."

Did she say something to me?

I do exactly what she says. I watch the ball as hard as I can:

from Gwen's glove to the swing of her arm—down, around, then forward again. The ball snaps out of her hand and comes at me fast, but it's slower in my head. I see it. I think, *It's low, but I can hit it.* I swing and smack. *That felt so good.* It goes right past Julie Meyers, who plays first base and doesn't seem to want it as much as I do. She comes completely off the bag to try to chase it down while LeaAnne runs to second—*safe*—and I run through first, *safe*.

I did it! It wasn't beautiful. It didn't sound great, but I did it. I hit the ball and got on base.

How hard is that? Not very.

LeaAnne claps for me. Coach, standing beside me at first base, says, "Good job, Ella."

Even the construction workers up on their perch cheer.

This is so fun. I LOVE SOFTBALL!

We go through our whole rotation and get two runs: LeaAnne the first, Mo the second. We're very proud, jumping around and laughing. I don't even care that Sally's the only one not celebrating. It's obvious she's the one who doesn't fit in. Even the starters tell us we did well.

In the field I play first base. Coach tells me where to stand and how to position myself when I'm waiting for a throw from third or short, left foot against the bag and right arm extended. The good lineup gets a lot of runs, though. Almost everyone gets on base, and the one fly ball that's catchable is a pop-up that I drop.

There are so many ups and downs in sports.

At the end of practice, Coach runs us hard. She sits on the bleachers blowing her whistle, scribbling on her clipboard. I'm almost hating her right about now.

And then this truck, a small white flower-shop truck, parks right where Sally parked that first day. A guy in uniform gets out holding a bouquet of yellow roses. He walks toward the bleachers while we're still supposed to be sprinting in shifts on the field. But because Coach is distracted by the delivery man, she forgets to blow the whistle for the next shift, so we stop to breathe and watch as the guy gives her the flowers. We're gulping air when she pulls the little card out and reads it.

After she does, she looks up at the Peyton Plastics building, where all the construction workers have gotten to their feet, taken off their hard hats, and stepped back a few paces to let one of their own come through. It's hard to see from here, but I'm pretty sure the guy that walks forward and takes a bow is Mack Elliot. And her reaction confirms it. She nods back and turns away so he can't see her smile, as if he could from that far away.

"Okay, girls, go home. Have a nice weekend. Stay out of trouble," she tells us.

Back in the locker room, Frannie and Mo invite me to a pep rally that's later tonight.

"For . . . the football team?" I ask, confused.

"No, that would be *every* Friday during school hours in the fall," Frannie says, pretending to be shocked by my lack of knowledge. "This is the tiny *one* they have for boys' soccer. Once a spring. But it is in the football stadium, if that's any consolation."

In Chicago, boys' and girls' soccer is played in the fall, and there aren't any pep rallies.

"We'll pick you up at seven?" Mo offers.

"Sounds great!" I exclaim, excited to have plans on a Friday night. I wonder if Nate will be there, but don't ask.

I grab my stuff in the locker room and race out to the lower school, where I see Rocky's little brothers waiting. I wonder if I should say something, introduce myself. But they take care of it for me.

"Hi, I'm Thomas," the older one says.

"I'm Ella. Nice to meet you."

"I'm Mikey. I'm eight."

"Hi, Mikey."

"Rocky says you play softball. Are you as good as her?"

"Not from what I've heard."

Their car swings around the loop and screeches to a halt in front of us.

"Cheese, you're gonna kill somebody," Theresa says from the front seat. She opens the door, climbs out, and gets in back grumpily.

"Nice hit out there today," Rocky says as I get in.

"Thanks." Then I turn to Theresa. "Are you sure you want to sit back there? I wouldn't mind."

"Whatever," she says, without looking at me.

"Theresa's cranky because she doesn't get her license for two years. Just ignore her."

We drive for a little while, and I give Rocky directions. But then there's a whole long stretch where she talks about practice. About the mistakes and the weaknesses. About how I can improve my hitting, catching, and throwing.

"I'm sure the coach would really appreciate your input," Theresa grumbles from the back.

I realize that I probably *could* use some help, even though it's hard to hear the bad stuff.

Rocky glances at me and smiles. "I don't mean to get all preachy."

"No, I'd love a personal coach."

When Rocky drops me off, Theresa gets out again and climbs in front. She doesn't even look at me, but it's hard not to stare at her because, even frowning, she's so pretty.

"Thanks for the ride."

"Sure," Rocky says. "See you Monday."

I practically dance through the front door.

Chapter 15

My mother is verbally trying to force a taco salad from my plate to my mouth. I keep telling her I'm not hungry. But we're both so excited I've been invited somewhere that she abandons the fight to get me to eat, and I abandon my wrath at being forced. Standing before the fridge in bare feet and wet hair, I drink a glass of milk and grab a handful of carrots to make her happy. I don't tell her about tomorrow morning's Safeway rendezvous for the Marriage Project—which she'll call a date. I have to focus on one thing at a time: what to wear to the pep rally.

The few weeks I've been here I've watched carefully the clothes kids wear to school, but I have no experience with the après-school attire. I call Christine's cell for help and leave a message. I call Jen, who's in the middle of an argument with her mom, and she says she'll call back. But time is of the essence. Amy's not much of a clotheshorse, so I skip her, and call my sister Beck in Boston. She's eating pizza with friends and puts me on speakerphone. Not the kindest moment in the history of sisterhood.

"Beck, I'm serious. I need to look casual and cool. But I don't want to stand out in any way."

Laughter erupts and I can do nothing but wait for her reply.

I'm desperate.

"Jeans and my old light blue tie-dyed shirt."

"Not tie-dye," someone groans in the background.

"It's a subtle tie-dye, just blue and white," Beck defends. And then to me, in a quieter voice off speaker, "That shirt looks really good on you. It's skimpy and faded and shows off your body. Seriously, it's perfect."

I'm momentarily shaken by the compliment. This is rare for us. But I take her advice.

When I come downstairs my mother glances at the outfit but doesn't comment. Dad hasn't gotten back from work yet and I'm watching the clock, hoping Mo gets here before he does.

"Beck recommended I wear this," I say.

I'm not asking her opinion and it's clear she understands that, when she says, "No later than ten thirty tonight."

I nod my agreement as Mo and Frannie pull into the driveway and run up the walk. They introduce themselves, bright and proper, to my mother, and I can see her relax a bit, relieved they appear to be good girls like Christine, Jen, and Amy. Mo looks adorable with her hair in pigtails and a Spring Valley sticker on her cheek, and Frannie's casual in jeans and a T-shirt.

We blast music in the car, not country western the way I pictured myself in cars with new Texas friends, but normal music—rock and rap. When we're five minutes from the stadium I can already see the lights beaming into the sky as if an alien ship landed across the street from school. The lot is packed, and cars line the busy boulevard so Mo parks in the teachers' lot, and we walk across the dark campus surrounded by kids of all ages, parents, even family dogs.

"I didn't think there'd be so many people," I say.

"They're getting primed for the fall," Frannie responds drily. "Don't mistake this as support for the soccer team."

Mo tries to soften Frannie's prejudice. "But at least people come."

"It's something to do in the off-season," Frannie says.

"So, you hate football?" I ask Frannie, thinking about the fact that Nate played.

"Not football, per se. It's the principle of the thing. Should anything at any school be this adored and overfunded? I don't care if you're in Texas or Hawaii or wherever; all sports should be equal. Boys and girls."

Mo says, "We have this conversation a lot."

"And I don't care if the football alums give a ton of money to the school. Good for them. Maybe if every athlete were treated the same, they'd all give money. Or maybe they already do and nobody remembers to mention it." She shakes her head. "No more football talk. Sorry."

"Agreed," Mo and I say together.

The stands are full of people wearing purple and green. It's hard to look at it for too long without shielding your eyes. The cheerleaders, Frannie explains, come out of retirement for this event and act put-out the entire evening. "They hang out with the football players until it's time to go on, and then they have to fake like they're into it."

Mo nudges Frannie. "I thought we weren't going to talk about football anymore."

"There's your boyfriend," Frannie says, pointing out Nate.

He's standing with a group of football players, wearing his jersey, which after tonight I'm guessing he won't put on again.

"He's not my boyfriend," I say, giving her a playful punch

on the arm.

"Sorry, *fiancé*."

I smirk but can't look away. I watch as his animated face gets swallowed up by a ring of secondary people—boys and girls, some from our Behavioral Science class—around the inner circle of broad-shouldered boys. I wonder if I'll have a chance to talk to him tonight.

We get caught up in the festivities—the school band, speeches by the headmaster and athletic director, an introduction of the spring coaches. I see Dixon and Coach side by side snickering like teenagers. Just as Frannie said, the bored cheerleaders get up and do their thing halfheartedly. Then the soccer team gets introduced by their coach, followed by a frenzy of cheers, and the team captain gives a speech littered with inside jokes and abbreviations I don't understand. Finally, a confusing muddle of grown-ups insists on congratulating the football players on their previous season. Frannie just grunts. The whole thing takes about an hour.

When it's over, we move slowly down from the stands, to the infield, where kids our age are milling around as if there's a destination, when there really isn't.

I literally bump into Nate without even knowing he was behind me.

"Ella Kessler!" he shouts.

"Hi," I say as he gives my sister's shirt an approving once-over. I'll have to remember to thank her.

"Big day tomorrow. Shouldn't you be home getting some sleep?" He winks.

Mo and Frannie stare at me. (And, if I'm not mistaken, a few random girls who are off to the side give me a good glare, too.)

I ignore the girls beyond Nate. "Do you know my friends

Maureen and Frannie?" I ask him.

He's the perfect gentleman. "I don't think we've ever formally met." He shakes hands with both of them and says, "I'm Nate Fontineau," as if there might be any confusion.

Later, in the car, Frannie concedes, "He's not too bad, for a football player."

Chapter 16

I tear through my entire closet trying to find another combination of casual, classy, and hip for my Safeway non-date, only to discover I shot my wad with the blue tie-dye. There's nothing left.

My mother, who I've filled in on the details, is carrying a laundry basket through the hall when she catches sight of the disaster. "Everything okay?"

"No!" I shout.

She laughs. "Oh, Ella, wear a black T-shirt, that faded denim mini, and black flip-flops. Clip your hair up; it looks prettier off your face. And wear a watch; they're so practical. Done."

I have to slam my door so she won't think her advice is worth listening to. Even though I do exactly as she suggests.

He arrives right on time. I can see him from my window, parking on the street instead of the driveway, running a hand through his hair as he comes up the front walk. And then I realize, horror of all horrors, that I'm upstairs and my parents are downstairs. The doorbell rings and my father walks through the front hall in his, *oh my God*, slippers.

The door opens, there's a conversation I can't exactly hear, and then Nate laughs. *He laughs.* I better make my move now. I take one last look at myself in the mirror—not bad—and fly down the stairs two at a time, tripping on the last three and sprawling there on the parquet floor at my father's slippered feet.

"And she's safe," my father yells, then kneels down.

"*Dad*." My voice betrays my disdain at his use of the baseball metaphor, and either I'm hallucinating, or he's wearing his slippers *and* his bathrobe. *Please, no.*

Nate says, "Are you all right?"

I stand up and brush myself off, try to be Frannie, and make a joke. "How'd I do?"

Nate and my father both beam at my mature ability to make fun of myself.

My mother comes into the hallway, looks at my outfit approvingly, and asks, "What's all the racket?" But before anyone can answer, she says, "You must be Nate. Nice to meet you." She sticks out her hand and he shakes it, looking her in the eye.

"We won't be long," I say to my parents.

"Could you pick up something for me while you're there?" my mother asks.

"Sure," Nate answers sweetly. Then, right in front of him, my mother gives me this look of approval and a slight nod. She may as well have just yelled, *What a nice boy, Ella!*

She hands me a five dollar bill. "Bananas and a bag of sugar snap peas."

"Okay," I say. "See you later."

We drive to the Safeway in silence until Nate says, "That was quite an entrance."

"Thanks. I practiced all morning."

He laughs again. I think Frannie is on to something.

I notice he's a very careful driver, which seems out of character, not that I know him that well, but he seems like the type to be roaring off into the sunset. When he comes to a complete stop at a stop sign, he looks over at me like he wants me to applaud. Even my mother doesn't do that.

When we get to the store he puts the car at the far end of the parking lot. "My dad always says to park far away from everyone so you won't get clipped." He shrugs. "It's about the only piece of advice he's ever given me."

I don't know what to say to that.

We walk in together and pause at the line of carts. "Should we get one?" he asks.

"Yeah. Let's just go crazy," I say.

He yanks out a cart and I reach into my back pocket for our shopping list and a calculator. "I forgot a pen," I say, irritated.

He leans over the cart and begins to push it into the produce aisle. "No prob. We'll add as we go."

"But how are we gonna record everything?" I'm a tiny bit annoyed; I mean, he didn't bring anything, not even a piece of paper.

He thinks about it. "I'll go up to the service desk and see if I can borrow a pen." And he leaves me there with the cart.

When he comes back he sees the bananas and sugar snap peas. "Look," he says all sentimental. "Our first groceries." And I crack up.

An hour later we're in the checkout line with our big cart and only two real items.

"Maybe we should get a Milky Way to fill it up more," I say.

"Definitely. And a Snickers."

At the register I pay for everything, including his Snickers, and put my mother's change in my wallet. Now I can throw everything into the plastic bag—our list, our notes, my calculator, my wallet.

"Here," I say, handing him the pen.

"Okay. I'll return it and meet you outside."

He comes to the watermelon bins in front of the store, where I'm standing eating my Milky Way.

"Hey, you started without me." He digs in my bag for the Snickers bar, and we lean against the bins, savoring the chocolate.

"Does $286.95 seem kind of high for one week's groceries?" I say.

"Not if we don't have to pay rent."

"Maybe we shouldn't eat meat every night?"

"We should clip coupons," he says.

"I can't believe how much cereal costs."

"I know. And milk."

I stuff my candy wrapper in the bag and notice my wallet's not there. I get nervous and try to remember where I last saw it.

Nate misunderstands my obvious look of panic. "Don't worry," he says. "We can eat mac and cheese until we figure out the budget." He's got this warm, funny, about-to-laugh smile, and before I tell him about my wallet, I think: *I could marry him for real*. But then I think of Sally and reconsider.

"I lost my wallet," I say.

"You just had it inside."

"I know."

"Okay, let's think about this." Then he basically takes control, the way my dad would. He asks what it looks like, did I put it in my pocket or my bag? What was in it? Could it have somehow dropped into the watermelon bin?

After a brief discussion, we lean over and carefully sort

through the bins until a manager comes out to give us a hard time. I'm mortified. Could they call the police on us?

Some lady comes up and asks if there's a problem. Nate says, "Oh, hi, Mrs. Pedicini," like it's nothing that we're here crawling around with the watermelons. "My friend Ella lost her wallet and we're trying to find it."

The manager seems uncertain what to do. People are starting to gather because surely this must be some health violation, two teenagers pawing through the produce.

Then Nate spots it. "I got it," he says as his whole arm disappears into a sea of watermelons. "Must've just toppled out of your bag."

"Are we all through here?" the manager asks.

"Yes," I say. "I'm really sorry."

As we head back to the car, Nate's about to hand over my wallet, but doesn't. "Wait a minute. When I asked you what was in your wallet, you told me 'nothing.'" He opens it. "But this doesn't look like nothing."

I groan. "Come on. It *is* nothing."

He rifles through my things, pulls out a card. "Chicago Public Library card issued to Eleanor Hamilton Kessler." He looks at me. "That's a pretty name, Ella."

I like his flirting, but at the same time I want him to stop. I don't want him to find anything embarrassing. I don't want him to ask me about home.

"No, really. What's Hamilton from?"

"My grandmother."

"Gotta love the family names. Oh, here we go. A Blockbuster Video card. And a business card: Jane Burrows Kessler, Advertising Sales Rep."

"My sister."

"You have a sister."

"I have three."

"*Three?*" he says.

Clearly one is enough for him.

"They're older. They don't live here."

We finally get to his car, which is really nice, by the way, nicer than the one that Sally drove onto the field the first day of tryouts. It's an SUV of some kind, black with darkened windows and a thin white line running along the side.

"Please give my wallet back," I plead, not really meaning to be so babyish or dramatic.

He unlocks the car and opens my door for me. A nice gesture if he wasn't holding my wallet hostage.

We both get in. "Millennium Park Skate ticket stubs?"

"From last Christmas. With my girlfriends."

"Ice skating?"

"Yeah. You've probably never heard of it."

He chuckles. "You know, we've got a professional hockey team in Dallas now. And we're doing better than your Black Hawks."

I still refuse to look at him, but I'll have to ask my dad about this later.

"And these would be?" he says, as he hands me a strip of pictures from a Navy Pier photo booth.

I look down. "Oh." I feel a little pinch of melancholy. "Yeah. That's Christine, there. And Amy and Jen."

"And who's the cute one?"

I smirk.

"Ahh. And here's eleven dollars."

"My life's savings."

He laughs and hands over the wallet. "That's not nothing in there."

"No," I say. "You're right."

We don't talk much on the drive home. In my driveway he leaves the motor running, and I know that whatever this was (*not a date*) is over.

"Well, that was good," he says. "Should we type up the notes?"

They're in my bag, of course. In my handwriting. "Sure," I say, which clearly means I'll be typing them up.

"Do you have a free period before Mr. D's class on Monday? We could go over our report together before we hand it in."

"I've only got lunch free."

"Okay. I'll find you."

"We could meet in the library," I offer.

"You don't want to be seen with me?"

I gasp. "No."

"Okay, okay."

"It's just we probably can't work well in the cafeteria." Plus, I don't want Sally to see us.

"Absolutely." He grins. "I get it. You want to be *alone* with me."

I open the car door and wonder for a fraction of a nano-second if he ever thought this was sort of a date, and if he did, would he want to kiss me? I lick my lips without thinking, then almost smack myself for being so obvious. How could I have done that right in front of him?

But he doesn't say anything, except, "Hope you're not mad about the wallet thing."

"No, it's fine. Really, it was more embarrassing to have lost it in the first place than to have you looking through it."

He stares down in his lap. "No, Ella. I mean I took your wallet out of the grocery bag. Just as a game. I was gonna have it magically appear when we got in the car, and then I'd look through it in front of you and ask you questions."

I'm staring at him.

"It was just a way to find out about you. Something fun to break the ice. You weren't supposed to notice it was gone, but then you did, so I guess I went along with it."

"And then you pretended to find it?"

"What was I supposed to do? Mrs. Pedicini was there and that manager guy."

I'm confused and feel a spark of fury in my belly. "I can't believe you did that." I snatch the bag of bananas and sugar snap peas off the seat.

"Wait. Why? Nothing happened."

"But I was embarrassed, and you thought it was funny."

He looks at me like he's really trying to figure it out. It occurs to me I'm not actually *that* mad. The store manager didn't call the police and there wasn't anything too revealing in my wallet. It's not such a big deal. But I can't find my way to telling him that.

"I'm sorry," he says, frowning. "I guess that was really stupid."

Now I don't know what to do. "I have to go." I get out and slam the door, not too hard to seem like a brat, but hard enough to seem like I've got my own ground rules and know who I am.

When I get inside, my mother is hanging up the phone. "Liz is driving me nuts with these wedding plans. Anyway, how'd it go?"

I take out our notes, hand her the bag, and say, "If $286.95 sounds like the right amount for one week of groceries, then I guess everything went just great."

I stomp up the stairs in a final attempt at drama and throw myself onto the bed. Mom follows me and sits down. She doesn't say anything, but it doesn't matter.

"Mother," I say into the pillow. "Leave me alone. For once."

She hesitates, then gets up and closes the door behind her. I begin to sob as I realize I've now overreacted to both my mother and to Nate. And I'm not sure how to fix it.

Maybe I need to review my playbook.

Chapter 17

Christine, Amy, and Jen call Sunday afternoon. They're near Oz Park listening to some awesome band I've never heard of, and I can hardly understand them, they're screaming so loud and laughing into Christine's cell.

"*We miss you!*" they yell together.

"I miss you, too."

"*How's Nate the Great?*"

"You'll have to ask him."

"*What?*"

"You'll have to ask him."

"*We can't hear you, but we love you. Bye!*"

And the line goes dead.

I'm so lonely my head hurts. I don't have any friends. Not really. Not ones that hang out in my bedroom and rehash every dramatic moment of the day. Worse, it seems like I can't even talk to my old friends, and it's not because of the music. Part of it is trying to describe my new life without making it sound better than my old life. But meanwhile, they seem to be getting along just fine without me.

On Monday I make it to lunch without seeing Nate. I've got our notes typed up and tucked safely in my folder. I skip the lunchroom altogether and go straight to the library. I have no idea if he'll show or not, but I find a table that looks out on the quad so I'll see him if he leaves the cafeteria.

I put my head down on the table for a minute and close my eyes, hoping for Nate to come, and for me to be able to say I'm sorry about how I acted. For everything to go back to normal. If there ever was a normal for him and me.

This is a big week. Our first game is Thursday, and I want to play so badly, but I know there's still a lot I don't understand about what happens on the field. I'm not sure it's possible to learn enough by Wednesday night, when Coach makes the lineup, to start Thursday. Maybe I can get Rocky to help me. Maybe she'll give me lessons.

When I open my eyes, I feel better. It calms me to think about softball, even though it fills me with nervous excitement, too. Softball seems like something I may actually have a little control over. Something in my new life that isn't impossibly complicated.

Then I see Nate on the quad with his friends. They're throwing a football around, because all boys in Texas throw footballs whether they played on the team or not, and a few of them gather along the sidewalk in a group, laughing and leaning in at something.

Nate breaks away from the group, trots over past my window, and disappears around a corner of the building. I stand up. Then sit down. Then turn halfway in my seat so he'll see me when he comes in.

He's out of breath as he enters the room and catches my eye. His face grins, the whole thing—mouth, eyes, scrunched-up nose. He lifts his open palm to wave. I wave back.

"I wasn't sure you'd be here," he says.

"I wasn't sure you'd come. Sorry about Saturday."

"It was dumb, what I did. I'm the one who's sorry." He sits down across the table from me, sees his buddies playing on the quad. Smiles.

I follow his eyes and ask about the guys huddled by the sidewalk. "What're they doing?"

He laughs. "Burning pennies."

I don't say anything for a minute because I'm not sure I heard him right. Then, "It's a game?"

"No. No, they just do it. You know, for fun."

Burn pennies? That's so random.

"Anyway, let's go over the notes," he says. And I think we're back on track. Sort of.

Practice is grueling. Coach breaks us up into infield and outfield. I'm with infield. Frannie and Mo (and Sally—thank you, Coach) are with outfield. Kat and LeaAnne, our catchers, go off to help with outfield, hitting fly balls and grounders to two separate groups at a very fast pace. I can see Frannie hustling between the two lines, joking around. I wish I were with them because they look like they're having fun. My group, on the other hand, is split up between starters and nonstarters. The starters take all the infield positions (except for catcher). And then the nonstarters get to be base runners. Oh joy.

We start off bunting—well, we simulate a bunt with a bat in our hands, since we can't be trusted yet with an actual pitch of an actual ball. No. It looks something like this: Gwen winds up and fake-throws the ball; I stand at the plate and fake-bunt the ball; then Coach tosses out a ball up the third-base line or the first-base line. And everyone scrambles. Coach yells out who is supposed to be going for the ball and who should be backing up first or covering third in case a runner advances.

Next we work on base stealing. From first to second, then second to third. Coach explains every detail of where each position stands, who backs up, and so on. She tells us where to go next if the ball is overthrown—which, thank you very much, it is. A lot. We runners get clobbered. Sometimes, if we run too fast, our batting helmet falls off and Coach scolds us. She says, "This is not about stealing bases. It's practice for the fielders so they know what to do in every situation."

That's nice, but not a great way to make the runners feel important.

Next: rundowns between first and second. Again with the wayward balls. How much of this are we expected to handle? Meanwhile, I could use a water break.

Midway through practice everyone gets combined again, and we learn sliding techniques. Coach has Kat demonstrate. First bent-leg, then pop-up, then hook, and last, the dreaded headfirst slide.

Coach explains, "This is the fastest slide but it has drawbacks."

"Like smooshing your boobs?" Frannie asks. We laugh.

"That, too. But also, it *can't* be used to break up a double play and lots of times that's exactly what you'll want to be doing."

I have no idea what she's talking about.

"Another reason is that the runner can't recover quickly enough to go on to the next base if that's a possibility."

I look around at nodding heads. Does everyone understand?

"And never use it sliding home because the catcher can block the plate," Kat says, swatting the dirt off her butt.

"Right," Coach says. "And that is dangerous for obvious reasons."

I can't follow any of this. But then we're moving right along to a grassy part of the outfield where Coach asks us to take off our cleats. Between the upper school and the library, my old friend Coach Dixon is driving a maintenance vehicle with a thick, cushy high-jumper's mat flopped over the bed.

"Being the assistant track coach has its benefits," Coach says. "Thanks, Dixie."

"Anytime, Coach." She unloads the mat. "Have fun, girls." Then she climbs back into her tiny truck and rides off.

We practice sliding for what feels like hours, much to the amusement of the construction workers. Maybe an audience isn't the best idea.

Finally we run the bases. Ten times with hardly any break to catch our breath. When it's all over, we basically limp off the field. At least I do.

In Rocky's car, I collapse onto the front seat, but she's full of energy. "Great practice today," she begins. "Wiped out?"

"Mm-hmm."

"But seriously, that was important information for you. Not the baserunning part so much. More the positioning of the fielders. You know, for hits and bunts and steals."

I can hardly look at her. Her enthusiasm blinds me. "Yeah. Sure."

"And you learned a lot."

I squinch my whole face up to silently question what she means.

She looks exasperated. "Look, every ball that's pitched, every ball that's hit, you have to know where to be and how to react. That's crucial for you defensively. Even if that ball is nowhere near you." She looks at me so long I'm afraid she'll drive off the road.

"Okay," I say.

"Okay? You mean, you get it? So, if you're playing first and the ball goes to left field and there's a runner on second, you know exactly where that ball should be going?"

"Uhhh . . ."

"Home. It'll be going home, but Debra Lester doesn't have the best arm, so she'll probably hit the cutoff, which *should* be Virginia Dalmeyer; she's excellent at third, but she's playing my position, so it'll go to Jenny Yin, since that's who the coach put at third today."

"You're confusing me."

Rocky shakes her head. "You're not trying hard enough."

"Yeah? Well, Virginia Dalmeyer's not playing *your* position anymore. That's *her* position. You're not on the team. Remember?"

Rocky's eyes are on the road and her expression doesn't change, but I know that I've probably said the worst thing I could say to her.

Theresa and the boys are noticeably silent in the backseat. I'm such a loser. Why did I say that? Why did I hurt her feelings on purpose?

"I'm sorry, Rocky."

"No." She looks at me, the shine gone from her eyes. "You're right. I'm not on the team."

"You're helping me so much. But it's hard to follow. I don't know half of what you're talking about. Or Coach. For instance, why can't a headfirst slide break up a double play?"

"If you're down low, the shortstop can still make the play, but if you're sitting up you get in the way."

I look out the window to process this.

"My guess is you were pissed about having to be a base run-ner for the whole practice."

"Not the *whole* practice."

"Okay, whatever. You've got to be good at that, too, you know."

"Coach didn't even want us to be good base runners. She told us we weren't the ones that mattered in these drills. What mattered were the fielders and the accuracy of the throws and catches."

Rocky's voice gets loud. *"And she'd be right. She's the coach."*

From the backseat, Theresa says, "Could y'all stop fighting. You're upsetting the boys."

"I'm not upset," Thomas says indignantly.

We hardly talk the rest of the way home. Now I'll have to tell my mother the car pool didn't work out, and she'll want to know a million details.

In my driveway I say, "Could you get out for a second so I can apologize properly?" I seem to be doing a lot of this lately.

"Don't worry about it," Rocky says.

"No, please."

"Fine." She leaves the car running, gets out, and stands in the front yard, hands on hips.

"I don't know why I said that. Everyone wishes you were on the team. It would change everything. Kat says we could domi-nate if you were playing short. And I could get good enough to play first, if you were there helping me."

"You don't need me," she says. "You only need to listen and watch."

"Isn't there some way, Rocky?"

She shakes her head and glances back at the car. "No. I don't play anymore."

"But . . ."

There's so much I've learned about Rocky from other people that I have to remember not to bring up her brother or aunt helping out since *she* hasn't told me anything.

"I gotta get going," she says.

I follow her to the driver's side. "What about throwing with me. At your house. You could teach me to throw better, like a girl."

Her eyes narrow. "You want me to teach you to throw like a girl?"

"A *real* girl. Like you."

She laughs. "I don't think so."

"You could help me learn about positioning and crucial defensive playing."

She shakes her head. "You don't know what you're talking about." She gets back in the car and slams the door. "Go take a hot shower. You'll need it. You're gonna be sore tomorrow."

She backs out of the driveway with a screech and tears off into the sunset. But before she makes the turn off my street, she puts her arm out the window and waves to me.

We're still hanging on by a thread.

Chapter 18

Not only am I sore on Tuesday, but Wednesday, too. Waiting to find out if Rocky will throw with me sometime this week and if I'll play against Fort Worth Country Day in our first game tomorrow makes the pain worse. Neither prospect looks too good. Rocky hardly talked to me the whole way home yesterday. And during the drills at practice today, Julie Meyers played first with the rest of the starting lineup.

I try to remember what Rocky told me. Listen to the coach and watch what the experienced players do. Try to be thinking about softball the whole time, not Nate or the fitting I have for a bridesmaid's dress for my sister's wedding or the fact that I seem to be off Sally Fontineau's radar at the moment.

But then I overhear Gwen and Joy talking about Sally's mother getting pissed off that Sally brought the car home late, since their BMW was in the shop. How many cars do they have?

Gwen says, "Her mom had to be at some fund-raising event downtown so she chewed Sally out for being irresponsible, once again. When Sally reminded her she was late because of softball, her mom went ballistic."

"What happened?"

Gwen shrugs. "She went on and on about how Sally wasn't

good enough to play in more than two innings last year, so why would she subject herself to that again? You know Mrs. Fontineau. We're not talking *Little House on the Prairie* here."

"God."

"I know. Then she told Sally how worthless it is for girls to play sports and that she should worry more about getting herself into any college that'll accept her so she'll have something to do after high school."

I stand there trying not to listen. I'm supposed to be listening to Coach. I'm up next in the three-player line-relay drill we're doing. But all I can hear is Gwen talking about Sally's mom. Nate's mom.

My mother would never say something so mean to me.

I'm in a rotation with Kat, who absolutely fires the ball at me. I catch it, turn, and whip it as hard as I can to Jenny Yin. Which isn't very hard. Or perfectly on target. But it gets there, and I trot off to get behind the last person in the next line. Coach is standing on the other side of the field, but she saw me catch Kat's ball. She saw me pivot and throw. She says, "Good job, Ella."

And this makes me very happy. What doesn't make me happy is the reading of the lineup at the end of practice. We're sitting on the bleachers passing around water bottles as Coach talks about the other team, their record from last season, their strong returning players. She talks about what we have to remember when we're batting and fielding. And then she reads the lineup: Julie Meyers is starting at first base. I get that sinking feeling, but then I have a reckless moment of hope that maybe Coach might have put me in another position—right field, possibly. But she stops reading, and I'm not starting anywhere in tomorrow's game.

I tried to prepare myself for this, but it's still a blow. Even though I'm not good enough to throw on target or smart enough about positions, I still had this crazy little hope.

Mo and Frannie accompany me off the field. They aren't starting, either.

"You okay?" Mo asks.

I nod, because if I speak it might come out squeaky, like right before I cry. They drape their arms around my shoulders to comfort me, and a small part of my frustration melts away.

Later, in the car, Rocky gets right to the point. "What's the verdict?"

"Julie Meyers is playing first tomorrow."

She nods. "You're gonna be better than she is. No worries about that. You'll definitely play, Ella. The question is, are you gonna *make* it long enough to start in a game? Because at the rate you're going, your disappointment will get the better of you."

I hear Theresa snort in the backseat. I don't respond. Neither does Rocky.

We drive all the way to my house, a good fifteen minutes before Rocky says, "Well?"

"I'm not gonna sabotage myself, if that's what you're asking. I'll be fine by tomorrow."

"Good. We can start our first lesson on Friday. After practice."

I climb out, sling my backpack over my shoulder, and glance through the windshield at Rocky. The sun bounces off the glass so I can't see her very well, except for her chin and the curve of her smile. I can't hold mine back, either.

Regular Season

Chapter 19

At dinner my parents ask annoying questions about tomorrow's game. I tell them I'm not starting, and the way they look at each other makes me realize they didn't think I would be anyway. Great.

They say they want to come. My father is even taking off work early.

"No. You can't."

"What do you mean? We want to watch the game," my father says.

"To see you win," my mother adds.

"That's my point. I probably won't play at all."

Neither responds to this. Finally, my mother says, "Ella, when I say *you* I mean the team. Watching *all of you* play. . . ." She lifts her eyebrows for emphasis. "You might want to think about that. It's called being a part of the team."

"Whatever," I say, stalking off to my room to bury myself in homework.

Thursday, game day, pours rain.

Frannie and Mo come up to me after fourth period. Mo says, "Can you believe this weather? On opening day?"

"I know," I say, as if I'm so upset. But after lunch the skies clear and the sun comes out strong, almost steamy. From my Spanish class I can see a little bit of the softball field where the maintenance guys are throwing sand over puddles in the outfield.

By Behavioral Science, word is that the game's on.

Nate gives me a brotherly pat on the back. "Ready for the big game?"

"Oh, yeah."

"Fort Worth Country Day," he says, like that's a complete thought.

"Right."

Mr. D hands back our food budget with a bright red A. Nate and I high-five each other, which causes a wave of eye-rolling by girls in the class. Nate never catches any of this. They're too careful.

The newest assignment, along with reading boring sociological data of marriage in different cultures, is a family tree. I have to complete one on Nate's family, and he does one on mine. The final version will be joined together. Another task I'll probably complete for the both of us.

Toward the end of class, during a lull, Nate says, "So, are you starting today?"

"You know it." I lift one shoulder and freeze that way. What did I just do? I can't believe I told him that.

He looks surprised for a flash of a second, but then he recovers and says, "That's so great. I'll come by after rehearsal and see if I can catch an inning."

Why did I say that? Did I forget that it's possible to be caught in a lie?

Nate doesn't seem to notice my horror. Instead, he starts

humming, which he's been doing a lot lately with *Show Boat* rehearsals heating up. It's a bit corny, but I like that he hums, even if it makes it hard to concentrate during class. Maybe it'll make him forget to come down and see me riding the bench in my spotless uniform.

In the locker room everyone dresses for the game in silence because the other team is here already, acting like they own the place. They stand at the long row of sinks and mirrors adjusting their hair and caps, perfecting their already perfect look: patriotic red, white, and blue uniforms, hair ribbons, shoelaces, and wristbands. We can't seem to stop gawking.

The Fort Worth Country Day coach has this husky smoker's voice and a kick-ass tan. She looks like she's been doing this for a hundred years, and you can tell by the way the team listens to everything she says that she's revered. The minute she yells, *"Time's up!"* they leap to attention and gather at the far end of the locker room in front of a small green chalkboard. It's almost creepy.

Coach marches into the locker room at about that time to get us psyched. When no one responds to her cheers, she says, "What's the problem here?"

"We're intimidated," Debra Lester whispers. "They're so big."

Which is true. They're huge. They look like they're in college.

Coach doesn't like this. She starts clapping and walks up and down the rows of lockers. "Okay, Lady Peacocks," she shouts. "Get proud and show me your colors!"

I cringe, especially since the other team can hear.

We shuffle out through the gym as ordered, but it's like she's forcing us to do something we absolutely do *not* want to do. The sun makes our purple and green uniforms explode, and I have to shield my eyes.

The starters begin infield, throwing the ball around from their positions when Coach hits it to them. They don't look half bad—until the Country Day girls appear at the top of the hill and descend in one massive red, white, and blue mob. The Lady Peacocks start dropping the ball, overthrowing it, missing it completely. Coach reels them in. She doesn't want the other team to see that we're nervous.

Their coach barks out, *"Infield,"* and the other team's starters dash out to their positions and hurl the ball around the bases, yelling and grunting at each other. They look so confident. *Thank God I'm not starting.*

After a minute or two, Coach comes over to the bench and crouches down to our level. She looks into our faces. "Don't watch the other team warm up; don't look so scared; and start giving your team some support. Send it telepathically if you have to. Believe it."

I happen to glance at Sally Fontineau. I've been avoiding this for a whole week, trying not to have any contact with her whatsoever. When she sees me, she rolls her eyes and pops her gum.

Coach notices the whole thing.

"Sally? Ella?" she says, making it seem like we're sharing some secret code.

I'm shocked. Surely she can't think I'm as indifferent as Sally.

But then, instead of reprimanding us, she says, "Hang in there. We're a team, remember? This is fun."

Sally looks at her fingernails. I look Coach right in the eye and nod my head, trying to project my I'm-a-worthy-part-of-the-team face.

Coach turns to go over the batting order with Sue Bee, and Sally says to me, "So, you took six after I took five?" She frowns.

I ignore her. Good comeback.

The umpires call for the captains from each team. Kat and Marcie go to home plate together while Coach stands by the bench. When Marcie comes back with our score book, she looks around and gulps, "They have a girl named Moose."

Sally's the only one who laughs.

Coach claps her hands to get us to stand at attention. "Okay, everybody, take a deep breath. We're doing it. It's happening." She looks around at all of our nervous faces.

Is it me, or did she linger on mine? Did she notice that I'm not as excited as I should be? Can she tell I like Sally's brother and that could be social suicide? Does she see that I lied to him and now I'm terrified he might show up? Can she read in my face, in my eyes, how much I want to play? But also how the other team is freaking me out?

Apparently not. Or if she does notice anything, she doesn't let on. She says, "All right, then. Let's give those Falcons something to talk about!"

Of course, Fort Worth Country Day has some predatory bird as their mascot.

The first inning is slow and brutal. Even though their number one batter pops out to short, the next three batters get on base with only one hit between them, a nice poke down the third base line. I have a thought that if Rocky were playing short, then Virginia would be at third, and maybe she would've caught the ball before it dropped in front of Debra Lester in left field.

Then I have another fleeting thought: *Maybe I* am *starting to understand more about the game!*

When the number five batter walks up to the plate with the bases loaded, everyone gets jumpy. Gwen's shoulders are slumped, which means she's already losing confidence in her pitching. Coach yells, "Come on, Peacocks!"

It's gonna be a long day on the bench.

Sue Bee, who's been telling everybody she wants to get into sports management in college, informs us that the number five batter is the girl named Moose. We're all quiet. Just as I'm thinking that she couldn't be named for her size because she's relatively small for their team, Frannie leans over and says, "She must have a huge swing."

And she does.

She knocks the ball over Nicki Porter's head in center field. Nicki chases after it, grabs the ball, and throws it to Virginia—but it's way off the mark. When the ball finally hits Kat's glove at home, Moose has already crossed the plate. A grand slam in the first inning.

Not a spectacular debut for the Peacocks. Even the construction workers are quiet.

I notice my parents in the stands during the third inning. I try not to look over because every time I do, they wave at me. And meanwhile, my mother is wearing this ugly polka-dot scarf that I've now decided is unlucky.

Please don't let Sally Fontineau find out they belong to me.

By the fourth inning, there are a few teachers and some other parents and a couple of girls I recognize in the stands. But no Nate, thank God. I wonder about Rocky, if she's watching or thinking about coming down. I see Mack Elliot hanging out by the bleachers, trying not to be too obvious. I keep looking at Coach to see if she notices, but she's just biting her lip through the whole game.

And it's pretty bad. Everyone's fumbling with the ball, chasing after it, dropping it, missing it altogether. It's embarrassing. Kat gets two hits, but the rest of the team never gets on base. After the fifth inning, with the score 14 to 0, the game's called. Slaughter rule.

I let out a deep sigh, not sure if it's because I'm relieved or disappointed. Nate never came. Probably he thought it would last a bit longer than it did. As it turns out, I'm glad I didn't play. I glance up at the library and wonder if Rocky will be able to help me at all.

Afterward we line up and "shake hands" with the other team, which I find out actually translates to slapping low fives. There's so much to learn in sports.

My dad comes over to the bench, trying to be upbeat. Then he introduces himself to the coach. I can't even watch. Please don't let him use any baseball metaphors.

My mother unwinds the scarf from around her neck, walks over to me, and says, "They were a good team. Tough."

Like she even knows what she's talking about. "Thanks, Mom. That's really encouraging."

"I just meant there's nothing wrong with losing to a good team."

Dad joins us. "What a nice girl," he says, about Coach.

"Dad, she's not a girl."

"She's not?"

My mother looks at him. "Try not to talk, dear. We can't say anything right."

I roll my eyes. "Thank you for coming. But I said you didn't have to."

"I think that's our cue," my mom informs my dad. "We'll wait in the parking lot."

We have a team meeting on the field. Coach is trying to fig-ure out what to say: "They were a good team. The best in our league. It's not so bad to lose to a good team if you look at it the right way."

I can't believe she just said the same thing as my mother.

"There's a lot we can learn from them," Coach adds.

And from behind me, Kat says, "You can say that again."

Chapter 20

I almost forgot about lying to Nate. Until Sally hunts me down in the hall before first period.

"So, my brother asked me how you played yesterday, you know, starting at first base?"

Honestly, she's heartless.

"It . . . was. . . ." How can I possibly explain?

"I'm sorry?" she asks, as if she can't hear me. Gwen and Joy are in the background, but they're not enjoying this. I see them so much in practice and they're usually pretty nice to me. But Sally never seems to notice. The whole thing is awkward.

"It was a mistake," I begin. "I wasn't even paying attention when he asked. It just slipped out."

"In your dreams," she says and busts out laughing. She stares at me for one more second and then shakes her head and walks away. Gwen and Joy shrug and follow her.

The rest of the day doesn't get any better. I don't have a chance to talk to Rocky. And I can't think of one thing to say to Nate that might explain why I lied. Sally must have told him. I decide the best thing to do is ignore it all. So I keep my head down as I walk into Behavioral Science and try not to look up the whole class. Luckily Mr. D spends the entire class explaining how the census works, while the girls that hate me pretend to take class notes when they're actually writing personal ones or twisting their hair into different styles.

It's Friday, the end of my third week at Spring Valley, but it feels like three years. How long does it take to be happy somewhere? To fit in and disappear into the woodwork?

Nate catches up to me as I'm walking to the locker room after class.

"Hey," he says. "I heard about the game."

My heart beats so hard I can't speak. I want to swallow myself up.

"Country Day is a powerhouse in every sport. Not a huge deal," he adds.

I stop and look at him. Tears burn behind my eyes. "I didn't start yesterday," I say. "I knew on Wednesday that I wasn't gonna be starting. I was really disappointed about it, even though I'm not very good. Anyway, I don't know why I lied. I think I wanted it to be true."

He frowns. "What did she say to you?"

Now, here's something I didn't foresee: that he might want to protect me from her.

"It's not a big deal."

"It is to me. And obviously to you, too, Ella. Look, you don't have to explain yourself. I get that you want to play."

I wonder if he'd "get" the fact that I wanted to play until I saw the other team. And that when we lost, I didn't feel like *I'd* lost because I didn't play, and therefore I didn't have to take responsibility. I smile weakly and tell him I've got to run. He looks like he might say something more, but doesn't.

• • •

At practice I'm back to square one; Sally snickers when she sees me, then whispers to Gwen and Joy. Frannie and Mo don't seem to notice, and I don't want to bring it up. Could this chain of embarrassment get any longer? I'm not even excited about playing softball with Rocky after practice today. I just want to disappear.

At five thirty, everyone leaves practice, and Coach calls me over.

I'm panicked. Maybe she thinks I've been slacking off or can see that my attitude needs tweaking. Maybe she wants to tell me I'm off the team.

"Hey," she says. "Everything going okay? School? You're making the adjustment?"

"Uhhh. Yeah." I hope no one is watching. I don't want anyone to think I'm getting special treatment.

"What about softball? You're liking it?"

"Yes. Of course."

"And everything's all right between Sally and you?"

Why would she ask me this? "Sure. Everything's fine."

"Would you tell me if there were some kind of problem?"

I hesitate. And for a moment, I really think about my answer. But then I notice that Mack Elliot has pulled his big black pickup truck alongside the field and is making his way toward us. Coach doesn't see him, but I do.

I try to concentrate on her again. "Umm, would I tell you if. . . ."

She feels him behind her, whirls around, and says, "Oh, you startled me."

I stand there smiling like a fool.

"Mack, this is Ella, from Chicago."

"Hi, Ella. Nice to meet you."

"You, too."

"Coach tells me you show a lot of promise as a softball player."

I almost say something, like thank you, but then it really sinks in that Coach, someone I respect, has told someone else that I show promise—and the feeling picks me up and shakes me loose. I start to giggle uncontrollably.

"That's enough trade secrets from you," she says to Mack, swatting his arm playfully. They've obviously come a long way from trashy fields and construction trailers.

As I walk back to the locker room, everything turns around again, from my first miserable moments in this new place to right now, right here, on the campus of a private school with peacocks roaming free, as far from Chicago as I could ever imagine myself. It's like I'm on an escalator in the mall of life—just when I'm about to hit the ground floor all stinky with fast-food restaurants and bathrooms, I get sucked back up to the top again, where I can look into the shiny windows of Lord & Taylor, Abercrombie, the Gap. Everything looks bright and shiny again.

Not too bad, if I can keep a good hold on the moving handrail.

Chapter 21

On the ride home, Rocky and I talk about yesterday's game. She asks me how it felt to be watching it from the bench. "I'm sure you wish you were in there helping the team."

"Actually," I admit, "I was glad I didn't have to play. They were so good."

She laughs. "That has to change. You need to believe you can help the team. But that'll come as you get better."

Rocky parks by a row of small houses that all look the same and have no driveways. We walk half a block with our stuff, and I don't say anything, but it makes me appreciate my new house. Rocky's door is blue; that's the only way to tell it apart from the others. We go inside and no one's home. The boys drop their backpacks and run to the kitchen. Theresa marches upstairs, and Rocky just looks at me: "Welcome to my world."

We walk outside to their backyard, which has two other yards on either side and stretches up against a long, high fence. Beyond it runs an alley and a stubby line of buildings facing another street, a busier one. It's loud and dirty here, and the grass in the yard is hardly grass at all.

Rocky says, "I just have to throw dinner in the oven and get the boys something to drink, then I'll be ready." She goes into the house through a sliding glass door, and I wait in the tiny yard, thinking how people's lives are complicated—whether they live here or in Chicago or Alaska. Things happen at home. Then you go to school and get on with life. And most people will never know the truth about your real life. Like that Rocky and her siblings could never afford our school if they weren't on scholarships. And that Nate and Sally have a mean mother, who apparently loves them unequally.

After a few minutes, Rocky returns wearing a T-shirt and a well-worn glove on her left hand. "Ready?" she says, smiling.

"Sure."

"Okay, all we're gonna do today is throw. We can talk about situations on the field; we can talk about yesterday's game; we can talk about anything you want, but all we're gonna do is throw."

We separate, and go to opposite ends of the yard. She holds the ball in her right hand, which I notice for the first time is really big. Both of her hands are. Huge, in fact. Not in a gross way, just in a way that makes the ball look like an orange instead of a grapefruit.

Her arm drops back behind her head and then she snaps the ball over to me, not hard, but forcefully. Directly. I can feel how she puts it exactly where she wants it: about a foot in front of my face.

"Don't think," she says. "Just throw."

"If I don't think, it won't go anywhere."

She laughs. "Yes, it will."

I try not to think, which is impossible, and plus I'm a little tired from practice, but also nervous to be throwing with Rocky. I try to let go and breathe, but I can't pull it off.

Rocky doesn't comment. She scoops up the ball from the dirt

and tosses it again, effortlessly, like she's swimming or stretching after a long nap. We throw back and forth for five minutes and the balls start to come harder, punching dust up from my glove. She's got this grin on her face, not at anything specific; it's just there. I'm beginning to see how good she really is, how much she loves this.

"Feels like you've been throwing all season."

"I haven't thrown in two years."

The ball smacks against my glove. "Really?" I stare at her.

She stares back. "Come on, throw," she says. And I do.

We throw for a good half hour, until the timer she set down by the sliding glass door goes off. "Dinner's ready. You wanna stay?"

I told my mom I'd be late, but said nothing about dinner. Also, Rocky and I hadn't really discussed how I'd get home after this little tutoring session.

"Let me call my mom," I say.

"Great. Phone's in the kitchen."

As I dial, Rocky sets the table and fills glasses with milk. She calls Theresa from the bottom of the stairs and gathers the little boys from watching TV in the living room.

"Mom," I say. "Is it okay if I eat over at Rocky's?"

"Tell her I can drive you home," Rocky says.

"Rocky can drive me home. Yeah. Okay. Thanks, Mom."

It feels like they're all watching me as I hang up. And suddenly I'm self-conscious about having a mother.

"Are you missing something good?" she asks.

"Not as good as lasagna."

"Ugh, we have it every other night," Theresa says, scowling. She's wearing shorts and one of the little boys' undershirts.

"No, we don't," Mikey says. "Sometimes we have hamburgers or pancakes."

Rocky shakes her head. "Theresa's right. Mostly I make dinners on Sunday that we eat for the rest of the week. Lasagna's easiest."

Instead of serving up the plates at the stove the way my mother does, Rocky puts the food in the middle of the table—the pan of lasagna cut up with a spatula, canned green beans, and a loaf of bread that the boys tear into pieces for themselves.

"Wow, this is amazing," I say.

Theresa busts out laughing at my admiration for the meal, and we all sink happily into quiet eating mode. By seven thirty we've done the dishes and cleaned the kitchen, and the boys are playing checkers at the kitchen table. Theresa lounges on the phone while Rocky looks at the clock above the fridge and says, "Anthony's usually home by now."

"That's okay. It's Friday; I'm not exactly in a rush."

We get comfortable in the living room, with me on the couch and Rocky on the floor leaning against a chair.

"How'd you learn to cook like that?" I ask. "I wouldn't know the first thing about making lasagna."

She shrugs. "It seems like I've been doing it forever."

"Doesn't Theresa help?"

"What do you think?"

I laugh. "I think no."

"Bingo."

I figure I have to say something about her mom, because she's never mentioned it, even though she drives her brothers and sister to and from school, makes the dinner, acts like the mother. And then there's the obvious, of course: no mother.

Finally I say, "I heard about your mom from Frannie and Mo."

She nods.

"I'm sorry."

"She was sick a long time, since Mikey was in diapers." Rocky sounds embarrassed to talk about it.

"How long ago did she die?"

"It's been four years."

When I don't say anything more she says, "My aunt used to help take care of us for a while, but now it's just us. And my dad, but he works a lot and Anthony works, too. It's actually fine."

Framed pictures clutter a bookshelf across the room. I point to a black-and-white wedding photo on the top shelf. "Is that her?"

Without looking she says, "Yeah."

I get up and cross the room. "She was really pretty."

"I know, what's weird is she got prettier as she got older." Rocky rolls onto her stomach and glances up at the shelves of photos. "But then she got sick. Cancer. And it faded the way she looked. But not completely."

I sit down near her. "Do you miss her all the time?"

She swallows hard. "Sometimes I feel like I'm forgetting her. How her voice sounded and how she looked standing in our room in the morning when she'd get us up for school. I miss her when I hear you talking to your mom on the phone asking for permission to do something. I haven't done that in a million years."

"I'm sorry," I say again.

"No. It's just what it is."

The front door opens, and the most gorgeous guy I've ever

seen walks into the room. He's wearing a uniform, like a cop or a paramedic.

"Hey, Rock." He stares at me with dark brown eyes. "Hi. Who are you?"

When I don't answer, Rocky says, "This is my friend, Ella."

He throws down his wallet and keys, sits in the chair Rocky had been leaning against, and starts to take off his shoes.

"I'm Anthony. You go to Spring Valley?"

I nod because he's so beautiful I can't speak. He's got short black hair and a dimpled chin, strong hands like Rocky, and a long, straight nose like Theresa's. Just taking off his shoes is this exquisite, excruciating event. I can hardly look when he pulls off his socks.

"Any dinner left?" he asks Rocky, even though he's still looking at me.

"Lasagna. You can throw it in the microwave."

"Perfect." He gets up. "Ella, it was nice to meet you."

"You, too," I whisper, trying desperately to act cool.

I remember the story Frannie and Mo told me about how he got hurt and lost a football scholarship to college.

On our way to the car, I ask Rocky, "What's the uniform for?"

"Security guard. But he thinks he's on *Cops* or something."

We laugh. I wait to see if she'll talk more about him, but she doesn't. At my house I say, "I really appreciate you throwing with me, helping out."

"We'll get more involved as we go along. The best thing right now is to get your motion down, make it second nature."

"Right," I say.

"Maybe you can find a place at home to throw against a wall, without breaking any windows." She smiles. "Work on stepping with your right foot and opening up your hips."

I nod.

She looks down at her lap. "You know, this might actually turn out to help me more than it helps you."

I don't say anything.

"I can't believe how good it feels to throw the ball again."

I look out my window at the pretty lawn, the bushes and flowers and bright red front door.

"Isn't there any way you could talk to Coach and have a special tryout for the team?" I blurt out.

She gazes at me. "It's not about the team or the coach, Ella. It's about my life." She pauses. "My father would never let me play. I've got too much to do at home."

"But you could still drive the kids home every day after practice."

"Yeah, but what about away games or Saturday games? There are too many things involved."

"Well, maybe my mom could help out. She doesn't do anything else."

"Like me?" Rocky rolls her eyes as if to say, have I taught you nothing? I forget how adult she has to be.

"You know what I mean. I'm the only one home now. My sisters are all out of the house. Maybe she could pick up the kids from school on those days. Or, what about Anthony?"

She doesn't respond.

"Doesn't he know how much you miss it?"

"Anthony does, but he's working. My dad has no clue. He's just trying to get some sleep between shifts. He never even saw me play. Of course, he never missed even one of Anthony's games, but that's football. That's Texas. It's a whole different ball game, ha ha. Besides, Anthony was a superstar."

"So were you, I heard."

She smiles. "I should get home, Ella."

I get out and wave good-bye, wait until I see her turn the corner, and then go inside through the back door. The house is quiet. I walk through the kitchen into the family room, where my parents are watching TV.

"Hi, Ell," my dad says. "How was your visit with your friend?"

He makes it sound dull. "It was good. We had lasagna and green beans and bread all in the middle of the table, and we served ourselves. It was so cool."

My parents look at each other.

"I'm gonna take a shower," I say.

In my room everything is in its place. Though I make my own bed, chores at my house are token ones, not like at Rocky's, where laundry, meals, and memorizing everyone's schedules are requirements for existing. The pile of clean laundry sitting neatly folded on top of my dresser is my life in a nutshell. I realize that missing old friends and a house and a city is not like missing a dead mother. And not starting in a sport you're still learning is not like losing your whole future because of a knee injury.

Being around Rocky puts my universe in perspective.

Normally during the week, I'm lazy and just pick what I want to wear from my stack of folded clothes, but tonight I put everything away. Tonight, I begin a new way of doing things at home.

Chapter 22

Monday's a bad day. I'm not starting in tomorrow's game. I haven't talked to Nate since Friday when Sally ratted me out and I had to admit to him that I lied. Then today Mr. Dominick gave us a lecture on marriage in America and how it's changed so drastically in the twentieth century. It's depressing and I wonder if my sister knows all these statistics? To top everything off, Sally makes a crack during practice about my number six jersey and how I'm a wannabe. I don't know if anyone even figured out what she was talking about, but I wanted to die.

In the car, Rocky tells me I looked better on the field today.

"Not good enough," I grumble.

"What do you mean?"

"I'm still not starting."

She frowns. "Ella, it's not about that. At least it shouldn't be. You're not ready yet. You're still learning."

"But I know as much as Julie Meyers. You even said so!"

"I said you're *going* to be better than her. And probably, as far as raw athletic talent goes, you're already better, but she played first base last season. She knows where to stand and how to find the bag when she's not looking. And all the other important stuff.

Do you really want to put yourself out there when you don't know that yet?"

"How am I supposed to learn? How am I supposed to get experience if I never play?"

She nods. "Good point. But give Coach time to put you in. She already noticed your throwing. I can tell."

I roll my eyes.

"No, really. She's watching you. You're her pet project. I swear, I know these things. I'm a master of observation."

From the backseat Theresa scoffs on cue. But as I get out of the car, I see her look at me—Theresa—and there's kindness in her eyes, a secret thank-you of some sort. And I realize there must be a part of her that appreciates Rocky's love for the game and the small role she's able to play in it now that we're becoming friends.

I don't know how it happens so fast, but by the end of the week, we're 0 and 3. The whole team is in a daze, including Coach. I'm making my contribution by continuing to throw with Rocky every few nights, and I'm getting better, my throw harder and on target. We've been using a cushion from the couch as first base. I say we should at least put it in a garbage bag to protect it, so we try that, but Rocky says it makes too much noise, makes it too easy for me to find it.

I work on not moving my left foot from the base while she forces her throws all over the place. It's hard, but after ten minutes or so, I start to get the hang of it. I even scoop up a few backhanders, and Rocky's so proud she has to run over and high-five me.

In school Nate and I are distant, if you could've ever called us close. He's still nice in passing, but he doesn't seek me out like he did the first couple weeks of school. Lately, the Marriage Project assignments have been solo acts, like interviewing a person with your job and creating a resumé.

The worst part is Nate hardly ever hums in class anymore. I don't know what kind of sign that is, but I don't really analyze it because I've got softball on the brain all the time now.

Tomorrow is our first Saturday game, and it's against St. John's in Houston. We have to leave campus at seven in the morning and won't get home until late. I'm so excited. I wish more than anything that Rocky could ride that bus with us.

As I get in the car after practice today, Rocky says, "Big day tomorrow. Road trip."

I don't mention that I'm not starting since I'd sound like a broken record. "I wish you were coming," I say, then wish I could take it back.

She smiles, though. "So, what've you got for yourself?"

"What do you mean?"

"Snackwise. What've you got? For the trip?"

"I don't know. Nothing."

"Nothing?"

Even Theresa sounds surprised. "Nothing?" echoes from the back.

Rocky says, "Hello, 7-Eleven." She screeches into the right-hand lane and makes a quick turn. We drive about a mile out of our way and pull into the packed parking lot of the nearest 7-Eleven.

"Okay, how much money do you have?"

I yank my wallet out of my backpack. "Three dollars."

Rocky glances at Theresa. "Pool it," she says. "She'll pay us back."

"I will," I say. As we push our way into the store, I wonder what I'm supposed to buy. Those energy bar things? Gross.

Thomas looks at me solemnly. "Skittles are my vote. You can pop them in, they last a long time, and they aren't messy."

"I like Skittles," I say. "One super-size bag of Skittles coming right up."

Rocky hands me sunflower seeds "for protein," and Theresa rolls her eyes and says, "Chocolate," as if it's obvious. I decide on Junior Mints.

"And what do *you* think I should buy?" I ask Mikey.

He considers it. "Milk."

"But how's she gonna keep it cold?" Rocky asks.

"A thermos?" he suggests.

"That's a good idea," I tell him. "But I can get milk at home. What should I buy now?"

"How about colored paper? Or Band-Aids?"

"Mikey," Rocky says gently. "We're goin' for snacks here."

I back down the aisle. "Twizzlers?" I say. "Chips? Oreos? Fig Newtons?"

He frowns and says, "You better watch out," his eyes wide.

"What's it gonna be, Mikey?" I say, still backing up—and then, *BAM*—I knock right into a stand-alone rack of beef jerky. It teeters back and forth for a second, finally deciding to crash to the ground, along with all the snacks in my arms. As I go down, I try to catch myself on a shelf of Twinkies and Ho Hos, but it gives way with my weight. So I fall, too. In slow motion, I see Mikey's face and Rocky's, their mouths round in shock. Oh, this is typical. Somehow in the ruckus, a person from the long line at the register turns and catches me with lightning reflexes. It's like a movie, except much more embarrassing.

In a movie, however, Nate would've been the one to catch me. Or Anthony. But in *my* life, it's a big trucker with tattoos on his arms and a long braid down his back. Nate, who I've just now noticed, watches this whole thing from farther back in line. Along with the holy trinity.

Forget embarrassing. Horrifying? Appalling? No word can describe it. There's beef jerky everywhere. The sunflower seeds have exploded onto the floor. The Skittles seem intact, but the Junior Mints are totally squashed. When I look up, the nice trucker is smiling at me, lifting me to my feet.

"Thank you," I say to him, as Nate steps out of line.

"Ella? Are you all right?" He starts picking things up, filling his arms with beef jerky and Hostess products.

Then Mikey and Thomas and Rocky appear at my side.

Nate looks at me like I've lost it, which maybe I have. "Ella? Can you hear me?"

"What?" I say, kind of making a joke.

Rocky and her brothers start laughing.

Nate shakes his head and laughs, too.

Gwen and Joy remain in line with Sally, who's smirking. But I have to say, in the middle of this ridiculously awkward and public incident, for the first time, I don't care about Sally. Because Nate's talking to me, and Rocky's my friend, and I'm getting better at softball, and I miss my friends from home, but they'll love this story. And I'll embellish it to the best of my abilities.

"I have to go," Nate says after a nanosecond of meaningful glances. "Do you need a ride home?"

"We don't have room," Sally whines.

He doesn't even give her the time of day.

"Rocky's driving me, but thanks anyway."

"We need to talk, okay?" he says quietly.

"Okay."

"Maybe tomorrow?"

"I've got a game in Houston." I love saying that. I sound so cool.

"Sunday, then. I'll call you Sunday."

Sally buys whatever stupid things she's buying and walks out of the store without looking at me. Gwen and Joy give me a nervous smile. Nate nods.

Suddenly it's just us again. The manager is really nice about everything and says we don't have to stay and clean up.

So, I spend nearly ten dollars on snacks. (I offer to buy the popped sunflower seeds and the squashed Junior Mints along with fresh packages.)

We're all laughing and talking when we get in the car, until Theresa silences everybody: "How do you know Nate Fontineau?"

Before I answer, Rocky says to her sister, "No, how do *you* know him? And why do you care?"

"Everyone knows him," Theresa says offhandedly. "He's hot boy on campus."

"No, he's not," Rocky says. "He's too nice to be *hot boy*. He's got way more to him than the average flavor of the month."

"How would you know?" Theresa asks, taking the words right out of my mouth.

Rocky doesn't answer.

"Well?" Theresa leans over into the front seat. But she's not asking her sister, she's asking me. "What's with you and Nate Fontineau?"

Rocky looks over. "Does it have something to do with you and Sally?"

"No. And nothing's up with me and Nate. He's just my partner in Behavioral Science." I feel like I'm always saying this to people.

"For the Marriage Project?" Thomas asks.

"Does everyone in the whole school know about that?"

"Oh, yeah," Theresa says, sitting back. "Lots of couples start that way."

Luckily we get off the Nate subject and laugh most of the way home as the boys reenact my food expedition: the backward fall and the trucker's graceful catch.

As I'm about to get out of the car at my house, Rocky says, "Anthony knows Nate from football. They're friends. And Nate was one of the only people who said something to me when my mom died."

"I didn't know that," Theresa says.

Rocky looks at me as if she really knows what she's talking about. "He's a nice guy."

This makes me like him that much more.

Chapter 23

The bus we're supposed to take to Houston broke down somewhere this morning, so now we're going to be driving in two school vans, which causes our dear coach to panic. She's talking on her cell phone to the athletic director, getting instructions and directions. Then there's word that Coach Dixon might be coming to drive one of the vans and lend support. All of us agree this has the makings of a most excellent road trip.

Most of the team is here already, lounging outside the gym, waiting to be told what to do. Of course, the holy trinity hasn't arrived yet. God forbid they don't have a chance to make their entrance. Maybe we'll have to leave without them. . . .

Frannie, Mo, and I sit up against the bat bags as I show them my snack stash. They're impressed, and I begin to tell them about the 7-Eleven catastrophe, giving the trucker only one arm. Just when I'm about to get to the good part, where Nate tells me how desperately he wants to talk, Sally saunters up. She stops right in front of us and glares down at me.

I can tell everyone has stopped talking to watch.

"I don't know who you think you are," she says, noticing the audience, loving it. "And I don't know why you continue to perform these little stunts in front of my brother. But you need to get ahold of yourself and quit stalking him or whatever it is you're doing. He's had enough. And, as his confidante, so have I."

Her voice, her posture, her wet hair hanging down on either side of her face—everything about her oozes cruelty. I can't imagine what I've done in my life to deserve all this anger. I can't figure out Gwen and Joy, either. They just stand there without really looking at me.

Then Coach comes to my rescue, yet again, coffee cup in hand, hair slightly askew. "Okay, girls, glad y'all could make it. Why don't you take a seat, and I'll let you know what's going on. We're running a little late, so I need everyone's cooperation here."

I hardly listen to what Coach says. It's drowned out by the ringing in my ears, the pounding in my chest. I can feel everyone trying not to look at me.

Coach Dixon shows up then, looking like she just rolled out of bed. We smile—me more than anyone else, because I'm trying hard not to act stung by Sally's wicked stinger.

Coach divides us into two groups, half to go with her and half to go with Dixon. Frannie, Mo, and I are together in Dixie's van. (Frannie has latched onto Coach's nickname for Dixon, per usual.) Sally and the hooligans are not with us. Thank God.

Before everyone separates and climbs into the vans, Coach pulls me aside.

"Ella, you need to tell me what's going on."

Her face is so close to mine that I see the freckles across her nose, the deep greens and blues of her eyes. Then I look away.

"Nothing, Coach. Everything's fine."

She hesitates. "Listen to me. I'm watching her and I'm watching you. I won't let this go on much longer."

"It's okay, really."

"No, it isn't. But stay focused on softball and have a good ride up with your friends. You may not be starting, but I'm putting you in at first today, so I need you to be ready. Here," she says, pointing to my head, "And here," she repeats, pointing to my heart.

And that's all it takes. My fog lifts. "I'm ready, Coach."

"I know you are." She pulls my cap down over my eyes and turns back to her van.

Frannie and Mo sit in the back. The other seats are mostly taken by ninth graders.

"How'd we get stuck with all you young ones?" Frannie asks playfully. I squeeze in next to them.

Mo says, "I brought treats, too. I was gonna save them for the ride home, but maybe we won't be hungry then, and I'm starved now. Here." She pulls out intricately wrapped, sliced cantaloupe and strawberries.

Frannie reaches right over and tears it open. "Thanks, Mo-Mo." She pops the fruit in her mouth. "Sally's such a bitch. I wish I could come up with something to shut her up."

"I can handle it," I say, though I'm not really sure I believe it.

The ride takes about five hours. I don't tell them what Coach said about getting into today's game. I just try to bask in the sound of their voices, their laughter, and the music on the radio, which Dixie keeps changing in the middle of every good song.

By the time we roll into the parking lot beside the field, St. John's team is warmed up and ready to play. Their bleachers are full of fans, and a sign on the outfield fence reads: ST. JOHN'S SOFTBALL ROCKS AND ROLLS.

We tumble out of the vans, and Coach gathers us into a huddle. "Okay, Dixie, Sue Bee, and I will get the equipment to the field. I want the rest of you to jog out together. Kat and Marcie, you run the stretches for a few minutes, then grab a partner and throw. We'll start infield after that. Make it look clean and sharp because they're gonna be watching—the team, the coaches, the fans." She looks around at all our faces. "Show them what you're made of."

No one says a word as we spread out in the grass. I peek over at first base, where I might be playing later, and I can't believe how innocent it looks, just a canvas bump on an otherwise smooth infield. While Kat leads us in stretches, no one groans or chitchats the way we usually do. Something feels different.

"All right, grab a ball and a partner, everyone," Kat says, and we obey as if she's the coach.

My arm feels magnificent. Strong. Loose. I'm throwing with LeaAnne, who keeps looking at me after I throw her the ball. "Ella, nice throwing," she says finally. And now I know for sure that today is different.

I'm not part of infield, but I watch intently as Coach hits to the starters, and the girls pick off the balls effortlessly then throw around the horn. Dixie's hitting fly balls from the first base line to the outfielders, and I see she's a pretty good softball player, too. She's praising the girls as they run in, retrieve the ball on the first hop, and get it back to her in one long throw. They look good. The whole team looks good.

I throw with Frannie and Mo on the sidelines, and I want so badly to say something to them about possibly playing, but they might feel bad that they're not getting in the game. And there's always the chance Coach won't put me in.

As the game gets under way, Julie makes two errors in the first inning, and I have a feeling today's the day my uniform gets dirty.

At the bottom of the third, St. John's is ahead 3–0. Our team is getting ready to go back on the field when LeaAnne and I get the call from Coach.

"Ella, you're goin' in at first. LeaAnne, you're gonna catch." Coach grabs Kat before she puts on her catching gear again. "I want you on the mound." Kat immediately hands over the equipment for LeaAnne to strap on.

I go get my glove, wishing I hadn't opened the Junior Mints last inning. I glance at Frannie, who made me do it, and whisper, "I shouldn't have eaten the whole box."

She laughs. "They'll bring you luck."

I make a gagging noise, and she and Mo snicker and give me the thumbs-up as I trot out onto the field.

My legs are noodles. My fingers are suddenly brittle and cold despite the heat of the day. Virginia Dalmeyer has taken out a practice ball, and as she goes by me, she says, "Kat gets a few warm-up pitches, so we'll toss the ball to you and get you warmed up, too, okay?"

"Right," I say casually, but I want to kiss her for explaining this instead of just hurling the ball my way and expecting me to know what to do with it.

One of the things you don't take into account at first base is your proximity to the rest of the team sitting on the bench. If I look over my shoulder, Frannie and Mo will be right there. And Sally Fontineau. But I don't look over my shoulder. Virginia calls my name, and I stand in the ready position as she tosses a grounder to my left. I try to backhand it and miss. It rolls beyond the bench, and Mo jumps up to recover it.

I take a deep breath. What would Rocky tell me to do? *Don't think*, she'd say, *just throw it. Do what comes naturally.* I throw it to

Jenny Yin, at third, who throws a nice easy ball right back to me. Then I throw to Joy at second. She throws me a grounder, which I easily scoop up while feeling for the bag with my foot.

I can do this. I know I can.

Kat's pitching is solid and steady. With her shoulders up and her back straight, she simply reeks of confidence. I try to act the same. And I notice the St. John's batter does, too.

Sue Bee walks the sideline with the score book. She calls out, "Number six batter, walked last time." She glances at me, nods. Treats me like everyone else, giving me the information I need. I could get used to this. *SMACK*. A hit, scattering my thoughts. It's headed for Jenny Yin as the batter barrels down the first base line— right for me. Jenny lowers herself to one knee, snaps up the ball, and in one fluid motion, flings it across the infield toward me.

I remember that I need to get my foot on the bag, put my glove out in front of me—open—and get out of the way of the runner.

But Rocky's right: It's better if I stop thinking and *do* something.

Before I know it, the ball's in my glove, the ump's got her thumb goin' south over her shoulder, Kat's yelling, "*Oh, yeah*," and the next batter's coming up to the plate.

I did it! My first out. All by myself. Sort of.

I *love* this!

With a fly ball to left field, followed by one of those solid hits that whizzes right to the pitcher's face—Kat easily puts her glove up to snag it—we're out of the inning. Three up, three down.

This is so cool.

Teammates on and off the field high-five me, despite the fact that I only had to make one catch. Frannie and Mo get up and dust off the bench before I sit down.

Kat pats me on the back. "Here she comes," she says. "Watch out."

I can't believe how good I feel. It's like the incident with Sally this morning never even happened. She's down the bench, stuck there, and *I'm in the game*.

By the fifth inning, we've held the score at 3–0, and Kat gets up to bat. She stands back in the box and holds the bat high by her ear. She waits on the first pitch, steps out of the box, taps the bat on each insole, glances at Dixie by first base and Coach at third, then steps back in the box. I've got to remember this. Imprint it on my brain.

At last, she whacks a triple down the left field line. Dixie's hopping everywhere, sending Kat around the bases, but Coach holds her at third, and she obeys the signal. The whole bench jumps up and down, screaming. It's the first time we've shown so much emotion. Even Sally joins in.

With no outs and Kat on third base, there are two more batters before me. My belly feels like one huge, monstrous butterfly. Surely someone can connect with the ball and send Kat home for our first run of the season.

Virginia's up next. She gets the sign for bunt and is successful on the second pitch. The ball hops out to the left of the mound. Shortstop comes in, digs up the ball, and makes a fake throw to first as Virginia kicks up dust to beat the throw. But then Short turns and plants both her feet like she's going to pick off Kat at third. Fortunately, Kat notices and doesn't take off for home—but she's a few feet off the bag.

There's a standstill for a second. I'm so anxious I get the hiccups.

And then Short fakes a throw, Kat strolls back to the bag, and we've got runners on first and third. *No outs!*

Center fielder Nicki Porter, our sixth batter, goes up to the plate and seems completely surprised by the first pitch. As soon as it hits the catcher's glove, the catcher rips off her mask and fakes a throw to second as Virginia steals. I'm so glad that wasn't me—I wouldn't have known what to do.

I'm standing in the on-deck circle for the first time in my life. I remember this scenario from practice: When you have runners at first and third, the runner on first always steals second, because the catcher's not going to risk the throw and give the runner on third a clean shot at scoring.

I can't believe I actually understand this!

I don't know if Nicki is thrown off by the play or what, but she swings and misses at the next three pitches. So now it's my turn. I'm supposed to walk up to the box. So I do. I'm supposed to look mean, slightly distracted. So I do. And then, I'm supposed to look the pitcher in the eye like I'm gonna smack the hell out of the ball. So I do.

I try to remember exactly what Kat does. She takes the first pitch (which means *don't* take the pitch; that took me about two weeks to remember). So I do this, too. I stand there all smug and let the first pitch fly by—a ball, luckily. I step out of the batter's box, just like Kat did. I tap my insoles with the bat, glance at Dixie, who nods at me like she has no doubt, and then I glance at Coach. She gives me a sign. I think it's "hit away," because what else could she give me? I don't know anything else.

The second pitch comes in low, and I swing. A huge swing. And I miss. Before the next pitch I repeat the whole damn thing. It seems to take hours—stepping out, hitting my cleats, looking around, stepping back. Is it obvious I have no idea what I'm doing? But here I am, waiting patiently, holding my stance, and then without thinking I swing big again, using my whole body, and there's this delicious *ping* off the bat!

I don't even know where the thing goes. I just hear everyone yelling, and I see Dixie waving me on. So I start running.

Kat waits until the ball drops over the second basemen's head and then takes off for home. Dixie has me rounding first, but holding until the center fielder overthrows to second. As I take off, Virginia scrambles for home, and the pitcher scrambles for the ball, not sure whether to throw me out, or Virginia. Coach gives me the signal to slide, both of her palms pushing for the dirt. *Oh, no.* I basically throw myself down, face and boobs first. A mouthful of red infield dirt. But I did it! I got a hit—two runs scored. I'm standing on second with a dirty uniform.

The whole team cheers and claps. They're high-fiving Kat and Virginia, whooping for me out here on my own. I make the tying run and in the end, we win 5 to 4. And even though I never got on base again, I didn't make any errors playing first, and I was at the beginning of the line when we shook hands with the other team.

Coach praises us in the dugout. "You were down, and you brought yourselves up again. That's a really hard thing to do with such a young team. Be proud of yourselves. You deserve it."

Walking back to the locker room, Frannie and Mo give me a group squeeze and tell me I played great, but something's different. I see it in Mo's pinched smile and Frannie's quick change of subject. I didn't ride the bench for the duration this time.

I shower and get dressed along with the rest of the players that got in the game. The people who didn't play change their clothes and fold their uniforms neatly.

As I sling my backpack over my shoulder, I think of Nate's comment about sports at Spring Valley, and although it may be true that coaches keep everyone, it doesn't mean they have to play them, not if winning is important. And in most cases, it is.

Frannie and Mo have left the locker room without me, and I have to run to catch up. They don't say anything and I don't, either. Is this how it's going to be?

In the van, I think of how Rocky might be able to help Frannie and Mo, too. Then we could all play together and be happy again. Except for Rocky, that is.

And that's when I decide it: I have to get Rocky back on the team.

Chapter 24

Suddenly I can't stop smiling, imagining what it will be like with Rocky playing again. She deserves to be sharing that amazing feeling out on the field—which is totally new to me, but something she must miss. Being out there, playing together with these other people, even some you don't get along with, working toward the same thing. I never knew how complete it would make me feel.

Of course, we don't talk about this in the van. We don't talk about softball. No one dwells on my hit or the fact that I got put in the game or anything like that. We just talk about girl stuff. Celebrities, music, hot boys, bad teachers, the stupid things our parents say. Frannie and Mo's spirits seem to have lifted.

As Dixie explains her philosophy on why the great musicians only use one name, there's a sound like a gunshot, except louder and fatter, like it happened underwater. Dixie grabs the wheel tight and steers us off the highway onto the shoulder. She starts to reassure us. "Don't worry. Everything's all right. I think the van blew a tire."

Ahead of us, Coach pulls off the road, too. Luckily it's a Saturday, and there isn't much traffic. She flies out of the van and runs toward us.

"Damn!" she yells, seeing our back tire. "Everyone okay?" she asks, ducking her head inside the van.

We tell her we are. She and Dixie check the tire damage.

Frannie cranks open her window. "How's it look?"

"Shredded," Coach answers miserably.

"Do we even have a spare?"

Turns out we do. Coach gets it out from under the van, and Jenny Yin says, "We just learned how to change tires in driver's ed."

"Good. You can help," Coach says. "Here's the deal, everyone. You may get out of the van, but I want you to stay in the grass away from the highway. I'm serious about that. Anyone near the road doesn't play the rest of the season."

There's a silence before Holly Keith says, "I have to go to the bathroom."

"So do I," another voice chimes in.

"You can run down the ravine and find a spot, but don't go far, and come right back."

We unbuckle our seat belts and push our way out as if the van's about to blow up. Coach goes to her van and tells them the same thing, then makes a call on her cell phone. After she hangs up, Coach joins Dixie and Jenny Yin by the side of the van where they start to take off the shredded tire. We all huddle in little groups on the hill at the side of the highway, talking and laughing.

Frannie, Mo, and I sit on top of the grassy slope that leads down to a drainage ditch, where some of the girls are hiding behind the trees and bushes going to the bathroom. We're watching Jenny wrench off the first lug nut.

Coach and Dixie leap around at the success of the second lug nut. They don't see, however, that in front of the vans Sally, Joy, Gwen, and Nicki are trying to wave down commuters by wiggling their butts toward the road. Cars and trucks honk as they pass, and one eighteen-wheeler pulls over. Coach and Dixie look up and give the same scowl. "Away from the road, girls. *Now!*" Coach yells.

"We're just trying to help," Sally calls sweetly. She and the others look all innocent.

The trucker gets down from his cab and is greeted by cheers from the team. "Can I help with anything?"

"Can you change our tire?" Debra Lester asks, fluttering her eyelashes.

"Absolutely," he says, taking charge.

"No really, that's okay. I think we—" Coach begins, but Dixie interrupts her.

"Thanks," she tells the trucker. "We'd appreciate it."

"Sure, darlin'."

Coach scowls again. We gather by the trucker while he loosens the remaining lug nuts and pulls off the shredded tire. Kim Adams comes up the little hill from the ravine and accidentally kicks the hubcap holding the lug nuts. It flies up in the air, then tumbles down the incline.

"Uh-oh," Frannie says.

Debra Lester gasps. "Oh, my God. The love nuts, the love nuts!"

And the trucker looks around to see if this is for real. But Coach and Dixie start laughing, and we all join in as we comb the grass for the missing "love" nuts.

We don't pull into the school parking lot until eight thirty at night. We're singing camp songs in our van with the windows wide open. Parents are leaning against the hoods of their cars, chatting, hardly noticing us. I catch a glimpse of my father talking to someone else's father, turning his head when he sees us pull up. He's wearing a cardigan vest over a short-sleeved plaid button-down shirt. His dentist look. It's fashion suicide, but for some reason it makes me want to run out and hug him, which is exactly what I do once the van is parked.

It's surprising to him but not unwelcome. He hugs me back and kisses the top of my head.

"I played, Dad! For four innings." I tell him I got a double and two RBIs (runs batted in). "And we won!"

"Honey, that's great. Good for you." He gives me another squeeze. "You're playing in the majors now."

I try not to let that corny little comment ruin things. I wave to Frannie and Mo as they get into Mo's car together, hoping things will go back to normal. They wave back and I follow my dad to the Blue Bomber—not proud to slide in beside him, but too tired to care.

Chapter 25

I don't hear from Nate on Sunday. I was secretly hoping Sally might have told him about my stellar performance in the game. I thought he'd call to at least tell me whatever it was he wanted to tell me last week in 7-Eleven, but he doesn't. Instead, the only phone call for me all day is from Rocky. It's a welcome distraction from my Behavioral Science homework, a listing of places I'd mail the resumé if I really were looking for a new job. Does this resumé stuff ever end? Homework at my old school was steady and time-consuming, but much more straightforward. Spring Valley is full of creative theory. It's exhausting sometimes.

"Don't tell me anything about the game yet," Rocky says. "I'm making Impossible Cheeseburger Pie; Love Boat Chicken, don't ask; and everybody's favorite, lasagna. I'm free at four. You want to throw and stay for dinner?"

"I want to talk," I say.

She's quiet on the line.

"I want to talk about you playing softball." I'm not sure if she's still there. "Rocky?"

"Yeah, I heard you. Maybe we should throw at your house, then."

"Sounds good."

When she arrives, I've caught up on most of my homework and am wearing shorts and a T-shirt.

My mom brings us lemonade on the patio as we throw the first ball. "Would you girls like a little break?"

"Mom, we haven't even *started*."

"No, it's great. I'm so thirsty," Rocky says, smiling at her.

And I'm momentarily ashamed for not appreciating my mom the way I'd promised myself I would.

"So, you may as well tell me," Rocky says, planting herself in a chair. "First the game, then if anything happened with Sally since 7-Eleven."

I decide not to mention Sally's latest attack. I talk about the game so that we don't need to talk about her. Besides, I still have some thinking to do on it, to figure out why she's so mean to me and how much it has to do with Nate.

We sip our lemonades, and I rub the glass pitcher with my thumb as if a genie might come out and grant us three wishes. I wonder what Rocky's would be.

"*You played!*" Rocky screams once I've told her the news.

"I did. And Rock, it was so awesome. I didn't make any errors. I caught the ball. I got people out. I got a double and two RBIs."

"Holy cheese. Girl, you've arrived."

I'm smiling hard, shaking my head in disbelief.

"So we won?"

"Five to four," I say.

"*Yawwhoo.*" She high-fives me with her glove and chugs the rest of her lemonade. "Let's throw," she says.

I hold off on talking about getting her back on the team. I'll let her loosen up, bask in my success, which is really her success, too. And then I'll spring it on her.

At around five fifteen she looks at her watch. "Oh, man, I've gotta get home. Actually, let me call Theresa first."

We go inside to get her cell and stand in the kitchen as she makes the call. "Mikey, can you get T?" She whispers to me, "She can't even boil an egg."

I'm not sure if I can, either.

"T, it's me. I'm leaving in two seconds. Can you throw in the Impossible Cheeseburger Pie? It's in the fridge. It's all ready to go. Just preheat the oven to three hundred and twenty-five degrees and set the timer for forty minutes."

My mother comes in. She says, "Rocky, would you like to join us for dinner?"

"Thank you, Mrs. Kessler, but I have to get home. I hope I can take a rain check on that."

"You bet," my mom says.

I walk Rocky out to the car. "You don't have to be so polite. You're making me look bad."

"You *are* bad." She pauses. "You know what I mean. You're so lucky. You have great parents."

I don't know what to say. "We never got a chance to talk about you and softball."

"I know." She gets into her car.

"I've got some ideas. I think we should talk to Anthony, and your aunt, and my mother. And . . . I think you need to tell your dad."

She shakes her head. "You've got all sorts of plans for me, don't you?"

"Rocky, it could happen." I keep my hand on the door so she can't close it.

"No. It's impossible."

"So is that cheeseburger pie."

She snorts. "Oh, please."

"What about if we just . . . try it? The worst they can say is no, we won't help you out for one month of your life. And then you wouldn't be anywhere different than where you are already."

"I'll think about it," she says, and my insides leap.

"You will?" I take my hand off the door.

"I will. I'll give you an answer tomorrow." She climbs in, puts the car in reverse, and backs out slow—for the first time. As if she wants to be more careful. As if she's precious cargo.

Chapter 26

Waiting for Rocky's decision almost obliterates everything on my radar. When I get to school Monday, my geometry teacher, Mr. Milauskas, stops me after class to congratulate me on Saturday's game.

"Thanks," I say.

He's sitting on the edge of his desk, leaning forward with a fatherly grin. "You know, mathematicians love baseball. It's a very . . . well, for lack of a better word, *mathematical* game."

I spot Nate standing in the hallway.

"Mr. M, you're not gonna bore her with the details, are you?" he calls out.

Mr. Milauskas drops his head. "Is that what I'm doing?"

"How could you ever think that?" I say jokingly.

By default, I join Nate in the hallway and try not to act annoyed that he didn't call.

"Sorry I didn't call." As if reading my thoughts.

"No biggie," I say.

"Congrats on the big win in Houston," he says, but he seems uncomfortable. Jumpy. "I want to tell you . . . not tell you, exactly, but explain. It's complicated. And my life is really busy right now. I've got *Show Boat* and college acceptance letters, and there's so much I need to do." His eyes squint like he's swallowed something awful.

"My life is busy, too," I say. "Tell me."

He steps back. I've said something he didn't expect. That I didn't expect, either.

"Oh," he says.

"Nate, I've only been here one month." I'm not sure what I mean by this.

"I know."

"I'm just trying to keep up in school and learn to play softball."

"I know." He sighs.

I look one way up the hall and he looks the other. I want to cry. Just roll up in a little ball in the corner and cry, because this is the first boy I've ever really talked to and now he's too busy.

I tell myself not to think, just *do*. "This isn't a good time for me to get to know you, right?" I ask. "That's what you wanted to tell me?"

He frowns. "No."

"What did you want to say, then?"

"Don't you know, Ella?" He's staring at me, his blue eyes burning into mine.

A second later, Mrs. Henderson, the headmaster's secretary, bustles down the hall. "Off to class, you two. Off to class!"

And the spell is broken.

During practice Dixie has her sprinters from the track team run down from the track to do a little cheer for us and then sprint back. They yell, "Way to go, Lady Peacocks," as they disappear over the crest of the hill. We love it and so do the construction guys, who continue to cheer for us like proud fathers whether we win or lose.

For almost two straight hours we drill hard, and then Coach surprises us by giving us the day off from conditioning. No sprints. No nothing. We're psyched. But she puts up her hands to quiet us. "Okay, y'all. I want to give you a little pep talk before I read tomorrow's lineup."

We wipe the afternoon's dirt from our brows, passing water bottles around as she waits patiently for us to get settled in the bleachers. Finally she has our attention.

"I'm very proud of our win on Saturday. You played well."

We clap for ourselves. Am I crazy or is she looking right at me and giving me extra kudos for my stand-out play? Okay, maybe not.

"There's something I want you to remember, though. I want you to carry it on and off the field. You are a *team*." She looks around at us. She lets that word hang in the air. "I don't care what your differences are. I don't allow any unsportsman-like behavior on my team."

Please don't single me out. Please don't single out Sally.

She continues, "For the remainder of this season, I expect all of you to carry yourselves like athletes. Look out for each other; stand up for each other. Be friends and be teammates. You're connected to something and you depend on each other. This is your chance to show the world how cool it really is to be on a team."

After a second, she adds, "We have a little over a month to go. It's not that long. Let's play like a team and keep winning."

Then she reads the lineup, and I'm starting at first base.

I AM STARTING AT FIRST BASE.

Frannie and Mo give me thumbs-up, but they leave ahead of me after Coach dismisses us.

In the car Rocky says, "You're starting tomorrow, aren't you?" before I can tell her.

I grin and she slaps me a high five. Theresa and the boys cheer from the backseat.

My own private fan club.

I don't mention any of the weirdness between me and Frannie and Mo. Instead, I throw Rocky meaningful looks that say, *What have you decided to do?* But she refuses to catch on.

At my house, she leaps out after me. "Hang on," she says.

"What's the verdict?" I ask anxiously.

"I may be crazy, but I think you're right."

"You're gonna do it?"

"I'll start with Anthony tonight. Practice on him. And then I'll call my aunt Rita."

"They've gotta be willing to try this for a month. Even Theresa."

"We'll see. Anyway, after family, I'll talk to Coach Lauer."

"That'll be no problem," I say.

"Unless there's some rule about not letting someone play late in the season."

"Same philosophy applies. If you don't try, you won't know. What about your dad?"

"Not ready yet."

"You or him?"

"Both?"

We give each other a gentle knuckle-to-knuckle, and I whisper, "Good luck."

• • •

During dinner my parents can't stop talking about softball. My father's so excited about me starting in tomorrow's game that he's practically drooling. He slaps the table. "What do you know about the other team? What's their record?"

I'm like, Dad, settle down.

Later, in bed, I try not to think about Nate. Or starting in tomorrow's game. Or Rocky's talk with her brother tonight. Or Sally's anger. Instead, I think about sailing out of Belmont Harbor onto Lake Michigan—my hand on the tiller, the wind at my back, the sail open wide.

Chapter 27

I see Rocky in the hallway after Spanish class. A teacher has cornered her by the activities board. I've seen this teacher corralling little ones from the library to the lower school—she must be talking about Mikey. How rude that someone would interrupt Rocky's day, the only time she doesn't have to act like the mother. It couldn't wait until after school?

I walk up and stand to the side of them, waiting for the teacher to finish. She's ranting about a fight between Mikey and a girl in class. Rocky glances at me and grimaces.

The teacher steps back. "Well, Racquel, I'll let you return to class. Do I need to call your father or do you want to take care of this at home?"

"I'll take care of it. Thanks for letting me know," she says quietly.

The teacher gives me the once-over and walks off.

I stare at Rocky wide-eyed. "Racquel?"

"Thank God Anthony couldn't pronounce it when he was a baby."

We start walking. "That teacher is such a loser," I say.

Rocky shrugs. "It's easier to talk to me than my father. Plus, they get immediate results. Whatever. It's better if he's not involved."

"Why? He's your father."

"He doesn't know how to deal with the disciplinary things. I mean, he used to. Maybe he's not around enough, you know?"

But I don't think I know. We stop in front of one of the science labs.

Rocky says, "This is me."

"How'd it go last night? Did you talk to Anthony?"

"Yeah. I'll tell you all about it at lunch."

In line at the cafeteria, Rocky and I shuffle down to the register with our trays. Frannie and Mo are already at a table by the back windows. I'm desperate not to add more tension to my friendship with them. "We can tell them," I say to Rocky.

She looks at me.

"You can trust them."

"It's personal," Rocky says. "I don't want everyone to know."

"Everyone around here knows everything anyway."

She groans. "Okay."

We get to the table and put down our trays. Frannie and Mo beam at Rocky because she really is a rock star.

"We've got some news," I say to them. Without looking at Rocky, I keep on, "Rocky is making arrangements with her family to try to play softball again."

After a pause, Frannie says, "May I be the first to welcome you back to the team?"

Rocky shakes her head and laughs. "Oh, please. We're a long way from that."

"So what happened when you told Anthony?" I ask.

"He was totally supportive. He acted like he didn't know this was a big thing for me. He's like, 'You only played in eighth grade, how could I know it was so important?' And I told him, 'Anthony, I played in eighth *and* ninth grade. I was good. The school paper wrote articles about how I was gonna be the future powerhouse.' Of course, he doesn't remember all that because he was being written about, too. Even in the off-season." She rolls her eyes.

"Anyway, he said he'd do whatever he could—rearrange his schedule, pick up the kids, whatever."

"Wow," I say. "That's great."

"He also said I should tell Dad immediately."

"Did you?"

She spoons yogurt into her mouth. "I called Aunt Rita instead."

"Mother's sister or father's?" Mo asks.

"Mother's," Rocky says. She nods at Mo like she appreciates being asked that detail. "She and my father don't exactly see eye-to-eye on things, and when she used to take care of us, they hardly spoke to each other. It was bad."

"So, what did she say when you told her?" Frannie asks around a mouthful of sandwich.

"She remembered everything. All about my games and how well I did. That it was the first thing that made me happy after my mother died. But she has her own family. She had to start being *their* mom again."

"Does she want to help out?" I ask, getting to the point.

"She does. She's really excited for me. But, she also said I have to talk to my father." Rocky stares into her empty yogurt carton.

"How about we talk to Coach? Get everything in place, and

then you can present it to your father knowing that you're just waiting for his green light," I say.

Rocky nods her head. "Okay. That sounds like a plan."

After lunch, I pass Nate on the quad with his penny-burning buddies. I try not to look at him, but I see from the corner of my eye that he's coming my way.

"Hey," he says, all out of breath and so alive that it nearly knocks me over. He's holding an envelope in his hand.

A letter for me? Did he write down whatever he wants to tell me?

"I went home for lunch today to pick this up. You know what it is?"

I shake my head.

"It's a letter from the director of admissions at Southern Methodist University."

"Oh." And then I get what he's saying. "*Oh.*"

He nods. "Yeah, I got accepted! I'm going to SMU in the fall." He's literally shining he's so happy.

"That's really awesome, Nate. Congratulations."

A soccer ball floats his way. He takes one step and effortlessly heads the ball back to the middle of the quad. Of course, he can do anything. "Gotta go. I just wanted to tell you," he says.

That's it? That's all he has to say? Does he want to be my friend or not? I mean, I never understood why he seemed so interested in me. I'm a sophomore. I don't know anyone. I don't talk in class. I don't have hip clothes. Was it just for the Marriage Project? There's no other explanation, I decide. So I wave as he goes back onto the quad. As I approach the doors of the upper school, I think I see him watching me, and it makes me kind of sad.

• • •

In the library at the end of the school day, with all my books spread out in front of me, I'm trying to mentally prepare myself for starting in my first game. It's scary. The construction workers will be there. My parents will be there. Even if I'd told Nate, he wouldn't have believed me, so I don't have to worry about him being there. But still, a lot of people will be watching. Some of my teachers might come. And Mack Elliot.

I pack up my books and whip down to the bathroom. Just as I'm about to pee, some girls come in and I get stage fright. The girls are in mid-conversation, and I immediately recognize Sally Fontineau's voice.

"Why would anyone apply to a college in the same town that he lives? *Who does that?*"

She must be talking about Nate, although I didn't know SMU was in Dallas.

"But you said your dad went there," Joy says.

"So? Does he want to please my father? That's even worse. He says he wants to get into advertising. Why? I don't know. I don't think he even knows what advertising is. And also, is there really a degree in advertising?"

Gwen and Joy laugh. I can hear them changing into their uniforms, pulling on their socks and cleats. They don't even get into a stall. They don't care if anyone sees them. I hold my breath, start to sweat, pray they don't hear me.

"And get this: After college he apparently wants to live and work in Dallas. *Dallas.* Doesn't he want to go somewhere different? Doesn't he want to see the world? Like at least Tulsa or Houston?"

"But Sally, he'll be around. Won't that be nice for you?" Joy says.

No answer. I don't try to look through the crack of the stall door. I don't want to see her reaction. But I think I can guess.

Even if he lives on campus she'll know he's there, close by, and she can get him if she needs him. And she does. Whatever's going on at home and in the rest of her world, it's too much for Sally to handle alone. I've figured out that much, at least.

I know the feeling. Not that I have any rights to Nate, but I've discovered that people can fall into your life, even if it's for a short time, and you might not be sure what they mean or why they appeared, but there they are. You can depend on them. Like Rocky. And Frannie and Mo. And Coach. I know I can count on them.

And it makes me understand why Sally can't say anything back to Joy. It's scary to need people.

Then, as fast as they came in, they grab their things and run off, leaving me undiscovered and late for warm-up.

 Chapter 28

We lose our game in the last inning. The good news is that I play the whole time and don't make one error. I get three hits, but unfortunately none of them count. So, Sue Bee informs me that I didn't actually *get* three hits. (I want her to explain, but decide to stick to my less humiliating online resources.) One was a pop-up, caught by the shortstop, and the other ones were grounders, and I got thrown out at first by the second baseman and again by the shortstop. I gave Short the evil eye but I don't think she noticed.

The clincher to losing the game was my mother. She arrived wearing that stupid polka-dot scarf she wore to the first game we lost. I told her never to wear it again, but she always forgets things like this.

After the game my parents come over. I say, "Mom, that's the bad-luck scarf."

She looks confused and then, "Oh, Ella. Sorry."

My dad goes off to talk to Coach like they're old friends. There's a line of people wanting to talk to her and shake her hand—parents and teachers—so my father gets into a conversation with Mack Elliot.

I stare at him, trying to tell him telepathically that he needs to

169

stop talking to everyone in the whole world. Just as I'm focusing on my father, my mother asks, "Why isn't Rocky playing? She's helping you so much, and she's really good." My mother watches me carefully. "Is there a reason she isn't on the team?"

"You mean besides the fact she doesn't have a mother?" I say this gruffly because I explained it the first time Rocky and I threw at our house.

"Eleanor Kessler, you will not speak to me that way. I'm asking a question, not insulting you. You don't have to be defensive with every response."

I can see her point. But I don't say so.

She says, "I know she has responsibilities at home. You told me all that and about carpooling her brothers and sister. I'm asking, is there any way she could play softball, too?"

My mother has this uncanny ability to understand situations. I hadn't planned to tell her about our scheme until Rocky had spoken to her family.

My father has his back to us. He and Mack Elliot point at the Peyton Plastics building, which has made considerable progress.

I turn back to my mother. "It's funny you ask about that."

"Why?"

"Because I think she should be playing, too. She used to, and she was a superstar."

My mother smiles as if she completely understands. "So, what's the plan?"

I can't believe I'm telling her this. I feel like I've hardly told her anything else about my life since we moved here. "Well," I say. "She's already talked to her older brother and her aunt, and they're going to help out."

"What about her father? What does he say?"

I raise my eyebrows.

"She hasn't told him? She *has* to tell him."

"Mom, I know. First we'll talk to Coach and make sure there aren't any rules against joining the team midseason. *Then* she'll talk to her dad."

"You know I'll help out, if you want me to."

I have that scratchy throat, stinging eye feeling I get right before I cry, but I keep it together. "Thanks, Mom."

I grab my glove and hat and start walking toward campus.

It's then that I notice Nate coming down the hill. He's not running, but he's walking fast. His hands are hidden in his pockets.

"Ella," he calls.

"I didn't know SMU was in Dallas," I say as we get closer, and this makes him laugh.

"Yeah. I'm gonna be around for a few more years." He looks at me. "What do you think of that?"

I don't say anything.

"Do you want to go to prom with me?" he blurts.

"*What?*"

"Prom. You know, school dance, pretty dresses, tuxedos. Would you like to go?"

"But, I—"

"I'm just so happy, Ella. I had a good day. And I'm asking you to prom so we can go on a date." He looks down in a shy kind of way. "We could go as friends if that's what you want."

"No." I shake my head. "I mean yes. I'd love to go." *Please, God, let my parents say it's okay.*

He smiles. "Really? I know it's short notice. It's also on the same day as your Fort Worth tournament."

"What Fort Worth tournament?"

He laughs. "Two weeks from Saturday."

"Oh, right. Right."

"At least it's close. I think Sally's going to the prom, too. And Gwen and Joy. So, you'll be on the run together." He grins as if this is possible. "You didn't tell me you were starting today."

"Your news seemed a little . . . bigger."

"Starting is big, too. Hey, I have to catch my ride," he says. "Say hi to your parents."

He waves as he jogs away and I wave back, sweaty and confused and dirty, but gleaming on the inside. I'm going to my first dance, and not some little Hearts Afire dress rehearsal of a dance, either. This is the real thing. The prom.

In the car, I can tell that my mother saw Nate and is dying to ask about him. But she holds off. My father says even though we lost, the team is really starting to play hardball, and then he goes on about the Peyton Plastics building, how the panels are almost complete—that means the workers won't be able to watch us anymore—and the fact that Coach and Mack are dating.

I sit in the back, numb from the whole day, thinking I need to call Christine, Jen, and Amy to tell them I'm going to prom. They'll scream and want to know what I'll wear and how he asked me and everything. I don't think I'm up to it tonight.

Dad pulls into the garage, and we all get out. In the kitchen, my mother unties the scarf. "I promise I'll retire this until the end of the season."

"What?" I say. "No. Don't."

"But I thought—"

THROWING LIKE A GIRL

"I changed my mind. It's actually not bad luck. It might even be good."

She smiles one of her shrewd smiles. There's no possible way she could know that Nate just asked me to prom, but she knows something. She always does.

Chapter 29

Later on, I work up the nerve to ask my parents' permission to go to prom, but my worries were unnecessary. I think by the fourth daughter and amid the planning for the first wedding, they're worn down a bit.

My father's reaction is to put aside the newspaper, take off his glasses, and grin. "Now there's a curveball out of left field. I like that boy. Good for you, Ella." As if I'd gotten accepted at my safety school, and he was assured that I'd be going to college somewhere.

My mother is enthusiastic but also her same, old practical self. "Oh, darling. What fun this will be. We have to get you a dress soon, if it's two weeks from now."

I text message the girls back home and there is a flurry of happy responses, but I can't seem to find time to actually talk to them on the phone.

On Friday at lunch, I plan on telling my friends, but I feel shy about it for some reason and decide to start with Rocky on the ride home today. Before that, though, I've agreed to go with her to see Coach during a free period.

Coach is on the phone when we get there. Dixie's in the office with two other guy coaches, debating results from the Rangers' spring training.

Coach sees us and holds up one finger to let us know she'll be a moment.

Dixie says, "Hey, Rock. Hey, Chicago, how you girls doin'?"

One of the other coaches chants, "Ro-cky, Ro-cky."

I don't know why this surprises me—that everyone knows her. Of course, they would. She's been here forever, her brother was a star football player, and she was a star softball player. For a while.

Coach hangs up. "Hi, Ella. And you must be Rocky O'Hara. I've heard a lot about you. What can I do for you two?"

"Could we talk to you privately?" Rocky says.

"Sure. How about in the athletic director's office? Mr. Hardy's in a meeting."

"You're not gonna close the door, are you?" Dixie yells as we walk in and Coach closes the door. Then a muffled, "But how am I supposed to hear what's going on?"

We laugh. Rocky begins, "Ella and I are trying to figure out a way for me to play softball this season. I wanted to know, before I talk to my father, if there's any reason why I wouldn't be eligible."

We're standing there in the cramped office. Coach sits on the edge of the desk. "Wow," she says. "Can you tell me why you didn't try out at the beginning of the season?"

Rocky takes a deep breath. "I have a lot of responsibilities at home, and it's made it hard to participate in after-school activities."

"Have those responsibilities changed?"

"No," Rocky says reluctantly.

Coach nods. "So, what makes *now* different?"

"I guess Ella does. She's made me see that I might be able to do this."

I jump in. "I think she's doing more than her share at

home. Her family can help out more. We've already asked them."

"What about your dad? He's a hard sell?" Coach obviously knows Rocky's background. Probably from Dixie.

"You could say that."

"I'd love to have you on the team, Rocky. From everything I've heard, you're exactly what we need. I don't know of any rule that prevents you from playing, but that doesn't matter if you can't convince your father. You need to talk to him."

"I know. Everyone keeps telling me that."

And so we leave with Coach's green light. Now we just need Mr. O'Hara's.

During practice I give Frannie and Mo the update, and we're content with the progress, although I'm still pretty worried about Rocky telling her father.

On the ride home, I decide to wait on the prom info. Rocky has bigger things to deal with.

When there's enough bustling in the backseat not to be overheard, I ask, "You gonna talk to him tonight?" as quietly as I can.

"I think so."

"Call me if you need moral support."

"Moral support for what?" Theresa asks.

I need to work on my quiet voice.

"For being your sister," Rocky jokes.

Theresa rolls her eyes, but she gives me a quick look, like she seriously wants to know if everything's okay.

I nod. But I'm not really sure.

Chapter 30

We split a doubleheader against Hockaday on Saturday. I play great and get two singles and an RBI. My dad thoroughly enjoys this and my mother, wearing the *lucky* scarf, keeps tying and untying it through both games. I'm worn out by the time I get home and fall asleep before dinner.

I don't hear from Rocky over the weekend so I call on Sunday night to find out what's happening.

Thomas answers. He says, "Hang on," before I even ask for Rocky.

"Hey, Ella." She sounds normal, not like she's been crying or anything.

"Have you talked to your dad?"

"Not exactly."

"*Rocky*. We only have four games left before the tournament. And then SPC."

I feel very cool using the acronym for our conference, Southwest Preparatory Conference. *Going to SPC* means you made it to the state championships. It'll be the most exciting thing I've ever done.

Rocky says nothing.

"Is everything going okay?" I ask.

"Depends on what you mean."

She's being very cryptic. I say, "What do you think I mean? What's happening with the plan?"

"I'll tell you all about it in school tomorrow," she says, and hangs up.

But I don't hear it from Rocky. First period, geometry, Coach stands in the doorway.

"Coach Lauer, to what do we owe this early morning visit?"

"Sorry to interrupt, Mr. Milauskas. Can I steal Ella Kessler for two minutes?"

In the hallway, Coach says in a whisper, "I'm sorry, but the whole thing with Rocky is off."

"What did she say?"

"She didn't say anything to me. Mr. Hardy called her father."

"How did he know what was going on?"

"Ella, he's my boss. He wanted to know what Rocky was doing in his office, and I told him."

"But—"

"I couldn't lie, Ella. I couldn't cover it up. Especially if we wanted her to play."

"But why did her father say no?"

Coach looks around the empty hall. She says, "Look, I think there's a long history here that neither of us knows anything about. The way Hardy said it to me was that Mr. O'Hara can't afford to disrupt things at home. He needs her helping out the family, not the softball team."

"So Rocky never got to tell him that Anthony and her aunt offered to pitch in?"

"Ella, stop. It's over. This is a complicated family matter and we're not part of it."

"But she didn't get to tell him why this is so important to her. It's not fair that she doesn't get to do anything fun in her life. Does he really want her to be unhappy?"

"Oh, Ella." Coach looks torn. "You need to get back to class. I'll see you at practice."

I can't find Rocky anywhere. At lunch, I see Theresa across the cafeteria and rush over.

"I heard what happened. Where's Rocky? Is she okay?"

She stares at me. "You should've told me about your plan. You could've trusted me. At least, I could've prepared him for finding out."

"But why is this such a big deal? I don't get it."

"You don't know my father," she says, looking off beyond me. "Ever since my mother died he's just been . . . empty. He's the one who really needs Rocky, not us."

"Does she still want to drive me after school?"

"Of course. You're like her best friend. Just give her time to get over this."

I can barely get through the rest of the day. Classes drag on. I hardly ever see Nate during the day anymore. When I do, people always seem to be coming up to him with rehearsal information and last-minute changes. Even practice is slow.

When I get to the lower school parking lot after practice, Mikey and Thomas look at me curiously, but don't say anything. It's obvious everyone knows now what Rocky and I have been plotting. And that we failed.

"Are you still talking to me?" I ask Rocky when she pulls up.

She smiles, but barely. "It's like I got the wind knocked out of me."

"I'm really sorry."

"Me, too. The worst part was how disappointed he was, like I was letting the family down by dreaming of doing something else besides helping take care of them."

"But he doesn't expect that of anyone else, not me or Anthony," Theresa says.

I'm surprised she's said this and so is Rocky. "Thanks, T," she says.

"I have an idea," I burst out.

Rocky glances at me wearily. "No more ideas."

"But Rocky, you never got to tell your side. Is there no part of you that wants to at least tell your father how important this is? He's already mad; what do you have to lose? There are only a few weeks left now. Today is April 29. Championships are May 17 and 18. How much do a few weeks really matter?"

"Ella, stop."

She's the second person to say that to me today.

Part of me wants to scream at her and another part of me wants to keep saying I'm sorry over and over again.

When I get to the front door and Rocky's still in the driveway, I know I have to give this one more chance. I stop and turn, and she's getting out of the car and running across the front yard.

"You're right, Ella! I have to tell him how I feel. For my own sake, I have to do it."

"You do?"

"What, you're doubting your own advice?"

"No. No. Do you want my help? Is there anything I can do?"

"No. I have to do this on my own. I should've done it a long time ago."

In the house over dinner, I tell my parents everything, and they listen without interrupting. When I'm through my father nods his head in approval. My mother's eyes glisten. "Ella, it was good advice you gave. I'm so pleased that you and Rocky have become friends and you're able to help each other out."

I lie awake in bed for a long time after that, trying to think about simpler things, like riding the train at night and swimming in Lake Michigan, coming up for air, feeling the sun on my face. But then I decide to think of Dallas memories instead, like getting asked to prom and playing softball.

I picture our stubby little field and the rickety bleachers. I picture practice, Coach and the team, even Sally Fontineau. I try to drop Rocky into the scene, throwing with me and Frannie and Mo. But it doesn't really work. So I create my own setting in Rocky's backyard, working on my stretch from first base, and then having dinner in their cramped kitchen, except I add Anthony to the table, and I'm being really cute and funny. Finally, after I've said good-bye and driven off in my brand-new Jeep, I trick myself into falling asleep.

Chapter 31

Frannie, Mo, and I plan an emergency meeting in the cafeteria at noon. Sometimes it seems like everything important happens at lunch. Out of nowhere, Rocky slides her tray onto our table. A grin spreads across her face, turns into a laugh, and her whole body vibrates with the laughter. It's glorious. Because I know what it means.

"He said *yes*. My father said I could play!"

We whoop it up, high-fiving one another. I give her a big hug across the table, knocking my milk over into my mac and cheese.

"So, tell us everything," Mo says.

"I did exactly what Miss Know-It-All over there said I should do. I told him I understand that he wants everything to stay the same at home. Because I want that, too." She swallows a big bite of her patty melt. "But I told him there's something else I really, really want. And I explained, the best I could, about softball. About how I'm really good and I want to play. How I love it so much. And then I told him everyone was willing to help if he would agree."

Her eyes well up. She sips her Coke for a second.

"He hung his head for a long time. And then, finally, he looked up at me and said he was sorry. He kept saying it over and over. He said he never knew."

"What happens now?" Frannie asks.

"I told Coach this morning and we told Hardy together. He called my father to confirm, then he said, 'I think this player needs a uniform.'"

"Things happen really fast if you're good, don't they?" Frannie says, and we all laugh.

"What number did you get?" Mo asks.

Rocky looks at me. "Lucky seven."

"No!" I yell.

"I know. It's ridiculous," she says. "But I want to be a part of the numbers parade."

On the field, Rocky moves like water or wind, more fluid than any player I've ever seen. I think it's what happens when so much athletic ability meets an overflowing happiness. Everyone notices. Everyone tries to act normal, to not stare. But the way she catches a ball from any direction, the way she fires it off, all of it is grace and power and an absolute understanding of this game. It takes your breath away.

We push hard in practice. It's as if we're stronger and smarter than we were yesterday. Coach's voice sounds like she'll burst out laughing at any minute. Even the construction workers, who've now been forced to sit on the second highest floor of the building to watch us, seem to notice that something's different. The attention and encouragement gets us pumped, as if each of us wants to show Rocky what we've got, even though she secretly knows every player's strength and weakness from watching in the library the entire season. Her ability to remember all this and anticipate and compensate at the same time amazes me. She is outrageously beautiful when she plays.

On the way home we just keep looking at each other and laughing.

Theresa rolls her eyes and says, "*Please.*" But I can tell she's happy for Rocky, in her own way.

All day Wednesday, I can feel the excitement of tonight's game thumping in my chest. I see Nate for five minutes and I can't stop giggling. He keeps saying, "What?" and he probably thinks I'm this way because of prom. I have no appetite for lunch, and when we're getting changed in the locker room, Rocky pulls out a stash of snacks for everyone.

Sally's in the background somewhere, grumbling and shaking her head, acting like she couldn't care less about anything. I just refuse to worry about her anymore because I'm in the game now. I hit and throw and catch. I concentrate on the other team. I listen to Coach and think hard about how to improve my play. I'm in it completely. And Sally's not. And, for the most part, that's her choice.

Before the first pitch, I see my parents introducing themselves to the O'Hara kids in the bleachers, and then sitting down next to them. Rocky sees it, too, and nods at me.

Out on the field, I'm nervous. The normal nervous for myself—that I don't mess up and that I hit the ball and don't wipe out trying to run the bases. But I'm also nervous for Rocky. She hasn't let on in any way, shape, or form that she's worried or uneasy. But it's been a few years since she's played organized ball, and with only one day of practice under her belt and a few weeks of throwing, I can't believe her confidence isn't a bit faded.

Of course, that would be me, not her.

Gwen's first pitch is a ball. Batter's calm. Second pitch flies over the plate. A strike. Batter's itchy. Steps out, in again, raises her elbow, narrows her eyes. On the next pitch the batter hits a hopping grounder between second and third, and Rocky dances to her right and scoops it up easily. She takes one step and fires it off to me. I catch it, ball slamming into my webbing. We did it! The team cheers, infield and out; the bench cheers; Coach cheers and the stands do, too; my parents and the O'Haras hug one another. And it's just the first out.

It goes on like this, mostly three up, three down. We all play better because of Rocky, but mostly it's her game. She's every-where—leaping, digging, sliding, falling. And that's only defense. At the plate, the other team's afraid of her. She puts the ball any-where on the field she wants. With a runner on third, she hits a blooper into right field, just over Second's head, getting herself on first safely and the runner on third home. Her second at bat, with no one on base, she smacks the ball between left and center field, putting her on second effortlessly.

By the end we win 4–0. The whole team runs together in a huddle of high fives and shoulder slaps. It's our fourth victory, and we're riding a surge of adrenaline with Rocky on the team now, knowing that we really are better than we were yesterday.

We line up with the other team to exchange *good game, nice game, good play, nice game*. Fans and parents and friends start to leave. The construction guys stand on the top floor, their hard hats off. Frannie, Mo, Rocky, and I wave.

With two more games before the Fort Worth tournament, which doesn't count toward our ranking in the championships, we have a chance to finish our season 6 and 5. Coach tells us not to project too far ahead, to work on the task at hand. So we don't talk about Saturday's away game or next Wednesday's last home game. Instead my friends and I brag about Rocky's game and how we're unbeatable and too cool for school. We talk about prom and the fact that Nate asked me (and my friends promptly scold me for the delay in telling them), and when I'm getting my dress, and how my parents feel about me going with a twelfth grader.

In the back of my mind, I list the happy moments in Dallas. I add this day, the whole day, and yesterday. Because instead of waiting for something to happen, like I've done my whole life, I finally *made* something happen. It's like in science class when you see those videos of flowers blooming in fast motion, the way they uncurl and stretch out in front of your eyes. I see that in my head, feel it in my whole body, and think I'm starting to bloom where I'm planted.

 Chapter 32

On the way to Saturday's game, Rocky and I end up sitting behind Sally and Gwen. These are nice buses, with bathrooms in the back and cushy, high seats, so I can hardly even see their heads, but still, for some stupid reason, I'm self-conscious about being this close to Nate's sister.

"I thought you were over all that," Rocky says, too loudly in my opinion. She can tell I'm squirming with Sally in front of us.

I give her an exasperated look and don't respond.

"All over what?" Frannie practically yells, although she and Mo are just across the aisle.

"Nothing," I tell them.

Everyone's listening to music, eating or drinking, talking about whatever. No one's focusing on me. But do they have to be so obvious? I can feel myself curling up again.

I've got softball in the bag in regard to Sally. But Nate is a whole other situation. I can't escape Sally completely because I'm still going to prom with her brother, unless she can sabotage that, which I wouldn't put past her. In the meantime, my friends have developed this absurd (what I would call, dangerous) fascination with the fact that Sally doesn't know yet that Nate and I are going together. This makes me very uneasy.

Luckily, the game isn't far away; it's in Arlington at Oakridge, and their record is worse than ours. So we arrive before anything bad can happen on the bus, and we're all pretty relaxed during warm-up. My worries about Sally dissolve as the butterflies invade my stomach; they appear no matter how often I play. Coach says it's all right to have a little stage fright before going out there. But mine feels more sickening than could possibly be good for me, or my game.

During infield, Coach notices our overconfidence immediately. She says, "Don't get sloppy, now. Have fun, but don't get sloppy."

I take deep breaths, blow out slowly. We're relaxed, not sloppy. Another deep breath. Exhale. We've got Rocky, how can we lose? Especially to Oakridge.

And we don't. We win by one run, which we get in the first inning. But Coach is steaming mad. After we thank the other team, she herds us into the locker room for a good reprimand. She paces back and forth like a caged animal ready to attack. Even Sue Bee seems disappointed, scowling at us with her sunburned face.

"I don't want to overreact here," Coach begins.

Sue Bee nods. She's getting on my nerves.

"You won. We're five and five. That's fantastic. But you played poorly today. Sue Bee, how many errors?"

Sue Bee glances down at the books, but you just know she already has this information on the tip of her tongue. "Sixteen."

"Sixteen errors." Coach looks around at us. At me. I made two. "That's sloppy. That's careless. That's cocky. And against a better team, that's a loss." She lets it sink in.

"Never underestimate the other team. I admit I did the same

thing. I walked onto their field and thought, *we're better than they are because they've lost more games.* But you know what? It doesn't mean I would've let my guard down on the field. They played well and you played like Rocky was our ticket to a Division I championship and like you wouldn't have to work hard. One player *does not* make this team. *Every* player does. The ones on the field, the ones on the bench. All of us together. If you don't get that, we are going to start losing again, for real."

The mood is somber on the bus. Sally and her gang sit way in the back and we sit closer to the front. I ask Rocky, "Did you feel like we slacked off?" I can count on her to be honest.

"Yeah. Me included. She's right. We can't let up. We've got to play hard if we want to win."

After a minute, she asks, "So, what're you gonna do when Sally finds out you're goin' to prom with her brother?"

Gwen passes our seats and glances wide-eyed at me as she continues up the aisle. She kneels down to ask Coach a question.

I could die. I could just die.

"Do you think she heard me?" Rocky whispers.

"Do I think she heard you? *Yes*, I do. How could she not?"

"Look, Sally's gonna find out anyway. I think it's interesting that he hasn't told her by now. But, you're over all your nerves about her, right? What's the big deal?"

"The *big deal* is that now she has plenty of time to think up some plan to humiliate me."

"Ella."

"What?" I say.

"Why are you giving her this power over you?"

"Rocky, I'm not like you. You'd never let someone control you. You never worry about what anyone thinks of you."

"Ella, look at me and my father. I couldn't tell him one of the most important things in the world to me until you showed me how. You have to face her and say what you feel."

"I can't. I can't think of the right thing to say when she totally obliterates me in public."

I look out the window as Gwen passes by again, and then say to Rocky, "The thing is, whatever I say to her goes back to Nate. She tells him I said this or that—anything she wants."

"So tell him yourself."

"Tell who what?" Frannie asks, leaning across the aisle.

"Nothing," I say.

We don't say much after that, just pull out homework and headphones. Back at school, I get off the bus as fast as I can and catch a ride home with Frannie and Mo, since Rocky has to pick up Thomas from a baseball game.

Looking out the window like we're being followed, I explain what happened on the bus. Only Mo understands the gravity of my situation.

"This is prom." Mo shakes her head with worry. "This *is* a big deal."

"But she's going with Nate, not Sally. Sally will have to deal with it. Forget about her anyway. She's going with that guy Froggy. Ella wins again." Frannie cheers.

"Brad French? She's going with him?" Mo sounds appalled.

"Who's Brad French?" I ask.

"Some friend of Gwen's boyfriend. Everyone's called him Froggy since about third grade. He's not a huge loser. But he's not like that guy Randy she used to date last year."

"What happened to him?" I ask again.

"He's dating some ninth grader," Frannie explains.

"I think Sally's gonna be mad at Nate for not telling her and she'll take it out on Ella, the way she has everything else," Mo says.

Frannie looks at her, then at me in the backseat. "That's right on, Mo," Frannie says. She looks at me again. "Hang in there; we'll think of something."

Somehow that isn't a huge comfort.

Chapter 33

Two days come and go. It might be a miracle, but I've seen Sally twice in the halls since the bus incident, and she hasn't even looked at me. Either Gwen didn't tell her, or she's waiting for the perfect moment to destroy my happiness.

I wish I could tell Nate what's going on with me. In class today, we get an assignment (a major holiday with the in-laws), and look at each other because we know we'll have to work on this one together. He watches me like he knows something's different with me today. But how do you tell someone you don't like his sister? Or that you're actually afraid of her?

As we work, I can't stop looking at Nate's hand. He's squeezing a pen in his fist, twirling it around, tapping it on the desk, twirling it again. "Okay, so, which holiday do we want to do?" he asks.

I hesitate. "Thanksgiving?"

"Good, good." He writes down *Thanksgiving*. I'm the one who usually does all the recording of ideas. His writing is nearly illegible.

"How's the play going?"

"Fine. We're almost there." He looks at me. "I know I've been busy lately. Are we still friends?"

The way he asks this, it's like we dated and broke up already. "Yeah. Do you still want to go to prom?"

"Of course," he says.

It's so awkward, how we can barely talk to each other all of a sudden.

And I wish I knew what it was, a million years ago, that he said he wanted to explain to me.

On Wednesday, we're standing on the field, Rocky at short, me at first, with Frannie and Mo cheering from the bench. The Peyton Plastics building shadows the field, closed up, no friendly faces calling down to us. At least the stands are full for our last game. After the top of the first inning, as Rocky and I jog in from the field, Frannie informs us, "He's not here."

"Who?" I say, wondering if she's talking about Nate.

"Mack Elliot. It's the first home game he's missed."

"What does that mean?" Mo asks the question we're all wondering.

"Bad vibes," Frannie concludes.

As we play, I look at the building only once, thinking about whether the construction crew will find out how we did in our last game, then I concentrate on the field. Holland Hall has a stronger defense than offense, so we're able to hold them from scoring until the last inning. They get two runs off good hits, and suddenly we're at bat, down by one run. We can't seem to muster the same enthusiasm from that first game Rocky played a week ago. And although she and Kat get on base, we can't do anything with it.

To say it's a huge disappointment would be the understatement of the season. First, the construction workers aren't there.

Then Mack doesn't show. We end up losing, and Coach doesn't even yell at us.

Rocky and I walk slowly to the locker room. Frannie and Mo are ahead, jabbering away about something. We just don't have the energy to join in.

"Losing sucks," Rocky says.

"Totally."

"Now that I've got my father into this," Rocky says, "he keeps asking me every detail, even though he can't make the games. I can't tell if he really wants to know or if he's trying to act as interested as he was with Anthony's football."

"I'd like to meet him," I tell her. "Is he coming to the tournament on Saturday?"

She shrugs. "I don't think so."

"Oh." We shuffle along. "I'm supposed to go shopping with my mom tonight. For a dress. For prom."

"Oh, no."

Just as we're almost to the safety of the locker room, Sally shows up. Her uniform sparkles, which you'd think would be somewhat embarrassing since Rocky and I wear the dirt and sweat of the game. But she flaunts it.

Sally gives me this glare, this full-on mean glare. "For your information," she begins, "Nate asked you to prom because he thought he should, since you're doing the Marriage Project and because you're new. If you want to get out of it, that's fine with him. Let's just say he wouldn't have any problem finding another date."

I should've seen it coming from a mile away.

Rocky takes a step toward Sally. She's more intimidating, even off the field. "What I can't figure out, Sally, is why you're so threatened by Ella. Is it that your brother actually likes her because she's sweet and kind and good-hearted and pretty and smart? Or is it because she walked onto the softball field and kicked your butt?"

Frannie and Mo come out the double doors with backpacks slung over their shoulders. Mo looks wary, but Frannie says, "Hey, gals. What's shakin'?"

Sally says, "You." And walks away with Gwen and Joy at her heels.

I look at Rocky. "I can't do this anymore, and I don't want you fighting my battles."

"But you didn't say anything."

"I didn't get the chance." I'm embarrassed and mad and just plain exhausted by Sally's unexplained cruelty. "I'm gonna shower and catch a ride with my parents," I say.

"Good luck looking for a dress," Rocky calls to me as I walk away, tears spilling down my face. I want to go back to Chicago, where none of this drama happened, where I lived my life pretty much unnoticed by everyone except my best friends.

In the car, my parents think I'm all torn up over the game.

"Nothing that a little shopping won't cure," my mother says, which makes me want to cry even more.

This is my first dance. My first real date. And nothing about it feels right. There are signs and decorations up all over school and girls talk about their dresses and dates in the bathroom, but I don't feel nearly as excited as I did the day Nate asked me. And I'm not sure why.

My father drops us off and parks the car. We get a bite to eat and he goes to Barnes & Noble while my mother and I start at Nordstrom. The first dress we pull off the rack is sea foam, a lovely confusion of green and blue. Two narrow straps go over my shoulders, and the dress gathers in folds at my chest, not so far down so that my parents won't approve, but far enough that it makes me feel pretty. It drops in layers down to the floor and rustles softly when I twirl.

There's no question. This is the dress.

"But, honey," my mother says. "Don't you want to look around more?"

"You don't think it's perfect?"

"Oh, love. It's beautiful. And so are you." She stands back. I can tell she's trying to keep it together and not overwhelm me when I'm already so emotional.

My father is even more surprised at the brevity of our shopping spree but certainly doesn't complain.

After we get outside in the parking lot, in the light just before dusk, the dress takes on yet another shade of shells and stones, like a chameleon, and I love it even more for this.

I call Christine when I get home. I want to talk about this weirdness with Nate, especially in light of what Sally said to me. But Christine chatters on about Amy spending so much time with Jen lately, so I decide not to mention it.

Over the next few days, my Dallas friends notice my bad mood. I barely say a word to anyone.

I spend most of the week avoiding Nate, but he catches me before practice Friday to fill me in on prom plans: He'll pick me up at seven, and we'll go to dinner; he hopes I don't mind we're not going with his friends. I can't seem to respond and he watches me carefully.

Am I trying to screw up my life before Sally gets to? Or am I distracted because I want to ask him if what she said was true, that he only asked me to prom because I'm new and we're doing the Marriage Project together? Finally I just nod my okay on the plans, and he waves as I head down to the field.

That night after practice, my mother comes into my room when I'm showered and putting on my pajamas.

"Ella, Rocky's here to see you."

"Oh. Okay. Thanks." I go down and she's standing in the living room. "I'm sorry," I blurt out. "About this week and how I've been acting."

She looks relieved, lets out a sigh, and crosses the room to hug me. "I'm sorry, too. For trying to fight your battles."

"No, you're being a friend. I really appreciate it. But it's like you said, I've got to deal with it myself."

She follows me into the kitchen, and I pull a carton of coffee ice cream from the freezer and two spoons from a drawer. We sit down at the bar stools and dig straight from the carton.

"You know," Rocky says. "I've been doing a lot of thinking since I started playing softball again. About my family and about how I ended up in this situation. My dad and Aunt Rita never really got along. They just sort of tolerated each other because of my mom. And the night my dad told her that we didn't need her help anymore, they got in this huge fight. My dad was acting really ungrateful, and my aunt was crying. They were out in the street yelling, and Aunt Rita said something I'm sure the whole neighborhood will never forget. She said that he never knew what he had. That he didn't deserve us kids, and he never deserved my mother."

"God," I say.

"I know. It was bad. I thought that would be the last I'd see of Aunt Rita. But she and Uncle Nick still came to all of Anthony's games with us on Friday nights. We still celebrated the holidays together. Life pretty much went on as usual. But I don't think my dad ever really thanked her for all that she did for us. I was thinking that if my mother was here, she wouldn't want things to be left unresolved like that. And I don't know, Ella. I guess I came over tonight because I wasn't sure if we were fighting, and if we were, I wanted to thank you anyway. For having faith in me and helping me face my dad."

"Wow," I say. "I guess I'll have to think of some way you can make it up to me." And I flash her a devilish grin.

She slaps my arm and my spoon goes flying across the kitchen.

"Hey, that's my throwing arm."

"Oops. Sorry. So. . ." She smiles. "Do I get to see the dress before I go?"

We tiptoe upstairs, and she stops in the doorway of my room. The sea foam dress hangs inside the clear Nordstrom bag on the back of my closet door. Rocky crosses the room to inspect it up close, but doesn't dare touch it. "It's gorgeous."

After we say good night, I lock up and go to bed. I need to get some sleep if I want to be ready for the tournament tomorrow. Everything else in my life will just have to find its place. I reach down for my glove on the floor, tuck it up by my pillow, and squeeze my eyes closed, memorizing the smell of leather and Spring Valley softball dirt.

Chapter 34

We arrive at Fort Worth Country Day well before our nine o'clock game and hit the locker room. There are a ton of other teams milling around the cavernous, well-lit space.

"All right, Lady Peacocks," Coach yells as she walks in, and we all cringe.

"We should tell her not to call us that in public, don't you think?" Frannie says.

"Meet in the field house in five minutes," Coach calls. "Bring everything with you, because we'll be going straight to the fields from there."

As we wander through multiple gyms and corridors on our way to the field house, Sally saunters in from another doorway with Gwen and Joy. And I feel nothing. Not fear, not anger—just distance. Like I can put her at arm's length, at least for this moment. I feel so much better than I did yesterday. Rocky and I talked. I slept well. I'm gonna play softball all day. And tonight I'll go to the prom, and even though I'm a little wary of Sally and unsure about Nate, I'm excited about getting dressed up and going to a dance.

As we sit down in front of Coach, she says, "We have one thing to do today."

"Go to prom?" someone says.

And I blush immediately for having the same thought.

Coach is serious. "I'm talking about this other thing called softball. Think we can manage that?"

We stomp our feet and clap our hands in response.

"That's right," she says. *"First things first!"*

"Wooo!"

"That's the spirit," she says, getting us psyched. "We've got a few games to play today, and we're gonna do it like we always do, one inning at a time. *Right?"*

"Right!" we yell back.

"Okay, quick review. Kinkaid has that pitcher with the double-jointed elbow. She was undefeated last year, but has been having problems, especially when teams start to hit away on her. So that's what I want us to do. Swing those bats. Look at me for signs, and watch me on the bases. Talk to each other, and let's hear a little chatter from the bench. Memorize the players and what they did at their last at bat. Think softball. Think smart. And blast the hell out of the ball. None of these games count against our record. But they count here." She points to her head. "And here." She points to her heart. "So let's win. Let's make this so much fun that we ride the wave all the way to SPC!"

That gets everybody riled up. We hoot and holler as loud as we can in the field house, and it echoes like we have legions of fans.

After a good warm-up, we're at bat, and we come out guns blazing. By ten fifteen, the ump calls the game and we win 6–0. Parents are on their feet cheering. Coach is smiling. She finds us a shady spot under a tree and keeps her voice steady and low: "You did it. You threw off that pitcher's game and that's all they had. Brilliant. Way to go."

We have an hour before our next game, and Coach forces us to come and watch the end of the Casady–St. John's game. "We play the winner of this game, so watch closely. Study the fielding and batting, talk to each other about which players to be careful of. Notice their strengths and weaknesses."

St. John's wins, and we head off to the cafeteria to eat our bag lunches provided by Spring Valley's cafeteria. Coach tells us not to fill up too much before the game.

"On school food?" Frannie says, pulling out snacks for the rest of us.

Forty minutes later, after warm-up and infield, Coach gathers us in the dugout and says, "I don't have a lot to add. You're on a roll. Hang on tight."

Coach tells us she's gonna be moving players around and putting people in. She says to be ready and I am. She reads Mo and Frannie into the starting lineup for the first time. Rocky and I cheer since neither of them have had much play this season. The four of us slap high fives before the first pitch and tap our knuckles together for good luck.

And Frannie, in her delirium at being on the field, yells, "Go, Lady Peacocks!"

We score three runs in three innings before Coach pulls me and Mo. Julie Meyers goes in at first, and Sally Fontineau goes in at right field. We beat St. John's 4–1 in a little over an hour. Frannie is walking on air after playing the whole game. My parents give me and Rocky big hugs. Then we run off to sit with the team.

"I don't know what to say, except—" Coach pauses as we pass water bottles around, wipe our faces, pull off our dirty socks and cleats. "You're looking good. We're in the finals!"

"Yahoo!" we yell.

"Let me read the lineup for the Fort Worth Country Day game. Then we can go cool off in the air-conditioning, okay?"

Rocky and I are starting, along with some of the ninth graders who haven't played all season. We're feeling great. Everyone seems happy, confident but tired.

In one of the many gyms, we haul our stuff into a corner and relax. Everyone's snacking and sharing music and talking about prom or finals, which are looming on the fringe of my radar screen. Frannie closes her eyes and leans back against the bag of balls. "This is the most uncomfortable pillow. So why does it feel so good?"

Coach comes in around three fifteen to tell us our game starts at four. We look at her blankly. She repeats herself, then says, "Softball. It's a tournament, remember?"

I can feel our fatigue, our sunburns, dehydration, boredom. We put on our stiff, dirty socks; our cleats and caps; and drag the equipment back out to the field, squinting against the sun.

In the huddle, Coach says, "Hey, hey, let's try to get excited! Come on, y'all. I know you're tired. It's been a long day, but you're young. You're strong. You're the 'fighting, fighting Lady 'Cocks.'"

We put our hands together and yell a rousing, "Go 'Cocks!"

Since Fort Worth Country Day has the most runs accumulated today, they're in the field first. As they trot out, they look as bright and fresh as they did this morning—their hair in place, their warm-up still fast and furious. Rocky and I exchange a quick look.

But we're at bat, and there's work to be done.

Joy and Virginia both fly out, Kat gets on base by an error, and

Rocky strikes out. Not a great beginning, but we hold them to a scoreless inning.

Still, we're lukewarm compared to the first two games. By the fourth inning we haven't really snapped out of it, and Rocky pulls me aside.

"How are we gonna keep up our energy and focus long enough to last two days at SPC?"

"I don't know," I say. "But let's play one game at a time."

She grins. Like it was a test, only it wasn't. "Good advice, Ella."

Rocky gets a double her next at bat, but I haven't gotten on base all game. I also don't have any errors, so I'm not complaining. By the start of the last inning we're losing by three, and I finally get a walk. On base I watch Coach, and she gives me the steal sign, which is touching her shoulder, shirt, or shoe, but it has to be "live," which means she must give an indicator first. (Otherwise, it means she doesn't want me to steal—it's only taken the entire season for me to understand this.) The indicator is fist to palm or hand to hat. I always hate this, because I'm never sure if I catch the indicator or not. And then if I do, I wait for the sign and get confused about that. If someone on the sidelines could whisper it to me, it would make my life so much easier.

This time, though, I take the chance that the sign is live and on the next pitch I go. Coach's words pound in my brain: *Don't turn your head; don't look down; run hard.* I do, and as the catcher throws to second, I go for the slide. I can hear Coach yelling, "*Down, down!*" I'm sliding on my butt, leg tucked under—it's clean—but the ball comes in right when I do. Not into the shortstop's glove, but bouncing in the dirt, then up into my mouth.

The pain is sharp and then dull. My eyes water and blur. The ump calls me safe and then calls a time-out. Coach comes running out to check on me and is followed closely by a trainer.

"Ella, you okay?" She brushes dirt off me.

"I think so." Already I can feel my lip inflating and imagine my mother freaking in the stands.

"Let's take a look at that," the trainer says. He holds my jaw in both of his hands and lifts my chin up like he's gonna kiss me or something. He's pretty cute, but way old, like at least thirty-five. "How does that feel, Ella? Does it hurt if I turn it this way?" he asks.

I shake my head.

"What about now?"

I shake it again.

"Okay," he tells Coach, "she'll have a fat lip, but other than that, she's fine."

"A fap lip?" I look desperately at Coach.

Her face reflects my horror. "It's prom night," she explains to the trainer.

They leave me out there on the bag. At least I'm safe. The team is standing on the sidelines waiting for the prognosis. "Just a fat lip," Coach yells. I can see Sally smirking as if this was part of her master plan. Then there's Frannie doubling over in laughter, and Mo smacking Frannie's arm in my defense. Only Rocky stands up and gives me two raised fists like I'm a hero.

I do eventually cross the plate. I am our only run. But we lose, anyway. It isn't slaughter rule this time. Four to one is pretty respectable, considering our first game against them five weeks ago.

After the game, the catcher says, "Sorry about the lip."

"No prob." I'm trying to be a good sport.

Her coach comes up, too. "Good game, First. Ice that all night and you'll be fine by morning. Ten minutes on. Ten minutes off."

I'll get right on that—as soon as I get back from prom!

After my parents survey my damage and decide I'm okay, I get on the bus and Coach counts heads. When the bus pulls out, Coach comes over and crouches by my seat. "You okay?"

I nod, barely. The ice pack on my lip has numbed my whole head.

"Look," she says, trying not to smile. "Only the coolest guys take athletes to prom. He's gonna love that lip. Trust me."

I ride back to campus in silence, because I'm tired and because no one can understand what I'm saying. I close my eyes and lean my head against the seat. I can't believe I'm going to my first dance, *the prom*, with a fat lip. I try not to think about anything else except the beautiful dress that's hanging on the back of my closet door with a little tag that reads, *color: sea foam*. And it helps to ease the sting, for now.

Chapter 35

Standing in front of the mirror in a towel, hair still wet from the shower, lip still huge from the game, I wonder if I can manage this: get dressed up, do my hair, eat dinner (with the lip), and go to the dance. I mean, I wondered the same thing before, like how would I talk to Nate with such a skimpy dress on, that sort of thing. But the lip adds a whole new dimension to the picture, literally.

My mother comes into my room. "Ell?"

"In here," I say.

When she enters the bathroom, I see the concerned look on her face in the reflection of the mirror. "Don't worry. It's going to be fine," she says. "You can hardly notice."

"*Mom.*"

She smiles as if she's trying to hold back the laughter. Seriously, she is, because when she talks, it's that bubbly sound you can't hide. "Honey, Nate's not going to care about it."

"You can say the word, Mom. You can say *lip*."

"Come on. I'll help you with your hair."

"I can do it. I'm fine. Really."

And so she leaves me alone. I turn on music and pull on my beautiful sea foam dress. My sister Beck would tell me to wear a robe and put the dress on last so I don't muck it up. But I decide to do it my way. It's time to establish a few more ground rules for myself. By myself.

Okay, so I might need some help with the makeup. I actually have a makeup case, which I got for Christmas when I was like ten. It came with all the fake kid stuff such as bubble gum–flavored lipstick and sparkly blue eye shadow. The red metal case looks like a mini tackle box, with a slotted shelf that lifts up when you open the lid. I've put earrings in its compartments, and they look like little fishing lures. The bottom part of the case has my makeup, only slightly improved from when I was ten: blush, mascara, eyeliner, and lip gloss. If Christine, Jen, and Amy were here, they'd help. If any of my sisters were here, they'd jump right in, too, though they'd be much bossier than my friends. They'd say, "*Ella*, don't do it like that." Then they'd impatiently do it for me, rather than show me how it's done.

Leaving the case on the edge of the sink, I go to my bedside table and call Christine. She's there, thankfully, because she's the only friend I've got in two cities who can help me with makeup.

"What's wrong with your voice?" she says.

I explain the situation.

"Oh, no." There's a long silence. "How much time do you have?"

We set to work, washing, moisturizing, covering up. Thank God there are no zits in sight. At one point, when I list the contents of my makeup case, she says, "That's it? I thought you were in Texas."

"Funny."

"Okay, okay. Let's keep going."

We skip the eyeliner since Christine says I'd do it wrong, anyway. Mascara on top lashes only. Blush on the "apples" of my cheeks (who knew my cheeks had apples?) and dusted onto my nose for a "sun-kissed" look. I don't tell her that all that playing softball has me sun-kissed for real.

Finally we get to the lip.

"Okay, is it top or bottom that's . . . fat?"

"It's top *and* bottom on the left side."

"Okay, apply gloss with care, obviously, dabbing on the swollen part. And then just roll your lips together if you can. Make the best of it. Act like it's an asset, not an obstacle."

"An obstacle to what?"

She pauses. "Sounds like you already know."

And we're giggling as we hang up.

It's nearly seven. I hear a car in the driveway. I peek out the window. Nate's too beautiful in his tuxedo. My mother rushes in. "Ella, he's here. Is that how you're wearing your hair?" She's practically hyperventilating.

"What's wrong with my hair?"

"It doesn't look like you've even brushed it."

"I don't brush my hair. I just let it dry. And I put some of this in it." I hold out a small bottle of what my sister Beck calls "product." "It calms your hair down. You might think about using it."

She says, "Very funny."

I take one last look in the full-length mirror on the back of my closet door. The sea foam looks grayish blue at the moment and matches my eyes. I put on tiny fake diamond earrings, and they work well with my tousled-hair look. All in all, as long as I don't rub my eyes and smear the mascara, and as long as no one stares at my mouth, I look okay.

My mother says, "Your father is going to take pictures of you and Nate."

"Mom, no."

"Yes. Ella, it's your first date, your first dance. You'll thank him later for taking a few pictures."

"Not with this lip, I won't."

She ignores me.

The dress swishes as I glide downstairs. Nate is leaning over my dad's shoulder to show him something with the digital camera. Then he stands up and sees me.

And I'm extra careful not to trip down the last step.

I've never seen anyone look at me this way—a long, wordless gaze like in the movies. I'm not sure if it's the lip or the dress or the fake diamond earrings that catch the light.

"Ella," he says.

"Hi."

We stare at each other for a minute, and the strangeness falls away. I can't believe how happy I am to see him. There's been so much going on with me and Rocky and softball, and, of course, Sally lurking in the background, that I worked myself into a panic over his intentions and whether I could safely like him or not. But here he is.

"I have something for you," Nate says, taking two long strides and grabbing a corsage from the table by the door. Opening the clear box, I see the pretty, purplish flower with baby's breath around it.

My mother says, "Oh, Nate, that's lovely."

"It's for your wrist. I wasn't sure if the pin-on kind . . . well, I didn't know if it would work with what you'd be wearing." He smiles.

I take it and slip the band around my wrist. It anchors me in a way. I tell him, "I got a fat lip."

He tries not to laugh. "I heard. Are you gonna be all right?" he asks.

I pretend to consider this for a moment. "I think so." The truth is, I don't even care about the lip anymore. I'm too happy.

"Okay, then," my father interrupts. "Three pictures. That ought to cover all the bases." He winks, and I roll my eyes.

When we're done, my father clears his throat. "Midnight, Nate."

"Yes, sir."

In the car, I say, "Sorry about my lip."

"Ella, please. That's crazy." After he starts the car and turns down the radio, he says, "You look really beautiful."

We drive slowly down the street. He keeps looking at me, smiling. Finally he says, "So I had this idea for dinner."

"Okay."

"Wait, I didn't tell you yet." We both laugh.

"So," he continues. "I used to bus tables at this diner. I know it's not romantic, but I thought it might be fun, and we'd get first-class service because I know everybody there."

"Sounds great." And I take a deep, relieved breath, because that's something I hadn't thought about: how to eat at a fancy restaurant without your mother there to tell you what fork to use or to stop drinking out of someone else's water glass.

The diner is a fifties kind of place with old-fashioned music and lots of neon signs. Frannie will love for me to describe it in detail because of her *Grease* obsession. I try to start memorizing things: the mini Coke bottles; the jukebox with Elvis songs; the waitresses in short, pink uniforms. A hostess takes us to a booth in the back, and various members of the staff come over to chat with us, waitresses and cooks and dishwashers. Nate introduces me, and they're all very polite, not mentioning my lip once.

Without looking at his menu, Nate orders a double cheeseburger, curly fries, and a strawberry shake. I decide on a hamburger, cheese fries, and a chocolate malt.

Then everyone leaves us alone to stare at each other. It's strange being here in our fancy clothes, but it's fun, and it helps me relax a little.

Nate says, "I know you've got SPC in Tulsa this weekend, so you won't be around for *Show Boat*, but I was wondering if you'd like to go to the dress rehearsal on Thursday night. It'll be like the real thing, except the seats won't be full."

Everything he says, every time he opens his mouth, my heart soars. I just can't get over the fact that he's talking to me, that we're on a date together, that we're going to prom tonight.

I realize I'm so excited I forgot to answer him. "I'd love to go," I tell him.

And then we start talking about the musical and how it's going. About softball and Rocky and how much I love playing and being on the team. He tells me he knows Anthony and how hard it was when he blew out his knee. We talk about Nate going to SMU in the fall and trying to be a walk-on for the football team. We talk about how good the food is here and how cool this place is. And we don't talk about Sally at all.

I feel like Cinderella, and I wish Prince Charming and I could stay here the whole night, because it's just us. Because he doesn't make me feel embarrassed about my lip or the fact that I've never been to a dance or worn a fancy dress. But it's nearly nine when we finish the hot fudge sundaes. He pays the bill and leaves the tip, and then there's no other reason to stay.

Back in his car, I say softly, "That was really the best dinner I've ever had."

He looks over at me, and says, "Me, too."

 Chapter 36

Prom is at the downtown Hyatt. We're almost there when Nate says, "I know things have been weird with you and my sister."

That's one way to put it.

"I've wanted to explain it to you for the longest time. So you wouldn't be . . . I don't know, scared off by her." He glances over to see if I'm still with him. "I know I give her a lot of slack, but there's more to it. . . ." He stops for a minute. Thinks.

I study my hands in my lap, the huge corsage on my wrist.

"My mother is pretty crazy and she drinks too much. And I barely see my dad. Sally seems to get everything dumped on her. I don't know how that happened. She used to be the princess in the family. Back when everyone was happy and my parents were still together." He sighs, like it feels good to say it. "If she didn't have me to stick up for her, she wouldn't have anyone." After a moment he adds, "Do you think that's messed up?"

"No," I say honestly, unable to imagine what life is like living with an alcoholic. I think back to the day I overheard Gwen and Joy talking about Sally's mom, and the whole picture becomes clearer.

"I have to look out for her," he says.

"I understand." And I actually think I'm starting to.

He reaches over and takes my hand. The corsage blocks my

view of our clasped fingers, so I close my eyes and just feel the warmth radiating up my arm. We don't talk the rest of the way, but he hums again and that makes me smile.

At the hotel, people are arriving in limos like it's a red-carpet film premiere. And the girls do look like movie stars bound up in their dresses and hair clips. The guys, though, still look like kids playing dress up. Except Nate, who drives us carefully through the chaos and parks far away from the fray. He grabs my hand to help me out of the car and holds on tight as we walk past people huddled in the parking lot, who are probably drinking or smoking before going in.

In the lobby a sign reads: WELCOME SPRING VALLEY DAY SCHOOL PROM-GOERS. I want to make a joke about how lame that is, but I don't. A nice lady directs us to a wide, winding staircase. She says, "You're in the second-floor ballroom."

Nate looks at me. "Is it that obvious that we're prom-goers?"

I just want to kiss him. I mean, not so much with my embarrassing fat lip. But come on, he said exactly what I was thinking. I love that.

Lucky for me, the room is pretty dark. It's decorated with fairy lights and two huge, dimmed chandeliers. We go to a table where a teacher asks for our tickets. Nate drops my hand to dig into his coat pocket, and I look around, feeling slightly unhinged. My chest and lip are thumping in time to the loud music.

In the few seconds before we disappear into the crowd of people, I wonder if I've truly changed since moving here. Then Nate takes my hand again, and we walk through the crowd, the huge wrist corsage bobbing between us, and I feel I've found something I lost a long time ago. Like a new sense of myself. A confidence I never had before.

I don't see one person I know. But all these guys keep coming up to Nate, slapping him on the back, saying hi to me, leaning into him and whispering. Maybe they notice my lip. Maybe not. It doesn't matter. He seems a little distracted by these interruptions and finally says to one buddy, "Hey, listen, Ella and I just got here and we haven't had a chance to get out on the dance floor."

And so, it's come down to this. Dancing is like singing for me. In the shower, in front of the mirror, I'm unbelievable, but would I ever sing in public? No way. I've been blocking out this part of the night, but now it's in my face.

I *do* know how to dance. I went to dancing school in seventh and eighth grade. I learned the waltz, the fox-trot, and the box step. But that's a big difference from an actual dance where I'm with someone I like and want to impress. And no one will be doing the fox-trot. There are no steps to follow here.

This makes my lip throb.

I guess he can tell. As Nate drags me out onto the dance floor, he says, "This isn't gonna hurt a bit."

But, actually, everyone seems to be having fun and making it up as they go along. Prince Charming, I'm happy to report, is slightly off the beat. He's actually kind of a bad dancer. I start giggling, and he nods his head, as if to say, *I'm the man.* Which makes me laugh harder.

But we stay out there for over an hour, and I realize this is what it's about, having fun, not caring if you're good or bad. We dance several in a row, fast and crazy, and then a slow dance. It's nothing like dancing school. My hands loop around his neck and his arms wrap around my waist, tight and warm. It's exhilarating because I can smell every part of him, his skin and his hair, even the heat from under his jacket. It's fabulous.

Then he steps back for a minute, holds me at arm's length. "The only thing bad about slow dancing is I don't get to look at you."

And my vast, puffed-up lip rises into a smile.

It's eleven when we take a break, and I can't believe the night is almost over. Will my parents be waiting up for me and will Nate kiss me good night with the condition of my mouth? I excuse myself and head to the bathroom to check my lip. It's packed with girls fixing makeup and hair, chatting and checking one another out. I quickly scan for Sally. Safe.

Hidden in a stall, I listen to all the voices. Do they even notice me at all? Not that I want them to exactly, because my experiences with being noticed by Sally and the girls in Behavioral Science have been disastrous. I thought coming to the dance with Nate and playing on the softball team might make a difference. But they don't seem to. No one's come up to me and said, "You play first base, right?" or "You're Nate's date, aren't you?" It's a bit disappointing.

There's a lot of turnover in the bathroom. So many girls and so many conversations. I decide to just enjoy this moment and not analyze it.

I take a quick peek at my lip, then I slip out. In the ballroom I look all over for Nate but don't see him anywhere.

Don't panic. He's probably looking for me.

I backtrack to the bathrooms, waiting casually, but don't see him. I feel a teeny tiny prick of adrenaline inside me. I try his cell phone, but he doesn't answer. I leave a bright message, trying to sound funny and not worried. Like I haven't been looking everywhere for him and asking complete strangers where he is.

It's eleven thirty. I pictured us saying our good-byes and walking out, arm-in-arm by now. It'll probably only take fifteen minutes to get home by the highway, but still. This is cutting it close.

Back in the ballroom, I weave through the crowd scanning every boy. I even look for Sally, Gwen, and Joy, my heart lifting and tumbling with every step. But no luck.

He's gone.

I don't know what to do. I can't call my parents. What would I say? Should I keep searching? Where would he go without me?

I walk out to the main staircase that sweeps down to the lobby. A beautiful, ornate clock above a fountain reads eleven forty-five. I stand at the top in my sea foam dress, on the verge of tears, when all of a sudden, a friendly face appears.

"Hey, Cinderella," he calls out to me. It's Anthony O'Hara in his security uniform. "Having fun at the ball?"

"Oh, yeah."

"Where's that Prince Charming of yours?"

"I'm not sure," I say, realizing how stupid this sounds. "I went to the bathroom, and now I can't find him anywhere."

He watches me descend. "Hope he didn't give you that lip."

I roll my eyes. "Softball. But what do you think about my dress?" I can't believe I asked him that.

"That's a given. Gorgeous." He smiles. "So, when's curfew?"

No, it's okay, I tell myself. We're not flirting. That's a nice, sensible big-brother question. "Midnight."

He glances at his fancy black watch with all sorts of scales and knobs and things, then down at my feet. "Cutting it kinda close. Still got both glass slippers?"

"Funny." But really I'm suddenly calmer.

"I'm off duty. Why don't you let me get you home. Nate can do his explaining later."

I look over my shoulder. Couples roam around and music

still pounds through the halls and lobby.

"Okay. Home would be good. Can we just check to see if his car is still here?"

"Of course."

I follow him outside, and it turns out he isn't parked too far from Nate, whose car is still there. I think of calling him again, but I already left a message. And why hasn't he called me?

Anthony shines a flashlight inside Nate's car to see if there's been any foul play, but everything looks normal. So we get into Anthony's car and drive out to the highway. I tell him where to go, but I don't say much else.

Just before we get there he says, "If it were anyone else, Ella. But Nate—don't worry; I'm sure there's a good reason for all this. Did you have fun at least, I mean, besides the losing your date part?"

"Oh, yeah. I'm Cinderella, right? I was the belle of the ball."

He laughs. And I smile because I never say anything funny.

When we pull in the driveway, it's five minutes after midnight.

"Parents gonna be mad?" Anthony asks, nodding at the dashboard clock.

"I have no idea," I say, because I don't have experience breaking curfew. I just hope my father isn't up peering out the window, wondering whose car this is.

Out of nowhere, Anthony says, "You've done a good thing for my sister, with this softball stuff."

I smile, the best I can with the lip.

"You let me know if there's any trouble, okay? With Nate. Anything."

I nod. "Thanks for the ride."

"Any time."

THROWING LIKE A GIRL

This isn't how I imagined prom night ending, but Anthony saved me from total humiliation. I have to be grateful for that, even though inside all my newfound confidence has broken to pieces.

My father's asleep on the living room sofa, glasses and an open book on his chest. I would love to sneak upstairs and not say anything to him about tonight. But instead, I kneel down beside him and kiss his cheek. "Dad, I'm home."

He sits up groggily. "How'd it go?"

"It was fun."

"Was Nate a gentleman?"

"Yes."

"That's my girl."

In the privacy of my room, I reluctantly take off the sea foam dress, not sure when I'll get to wear it again. Back in my usual T-shirt and sweats, I curl up in bed and stare out the window at the night sky. I want to cry. I nearly did at the hotel, but now, in the privacy of my own room, it doesn't come out. Everything seems so spectacularly wrong.

A *ping* against the windowpane tears me out of bed. I look out into the front yard, and there's Nate in his tuxedo, his hand raised up. At least he didn't completely forget about me. I have to know what happened, so I tiptoe into the hall and down the stairs. I open the door and he's standing there on the steps with a mix of relief and worry on his face.

"Ella, you're home safe. Thank God. How did you get here? I'm so sorry about tonight. I'm sorry I left. I mean, I didn't leave. I looked all over for you, but I couldn't find you, and I had an emergency. Or Sally did. She was in the hotel, in a room with all her friends. She kept calling me. I had to go up there. She was having problems with her date, but we got it worked out."

Of course, this is about Sally. She had to make sure I knew who was more important in Nate's life: her.

"You couldn't wait for me before you went up to check on her? You couldn't send someone in the bathroom to find me? I didn't know where you were! I didn't know what to do. I almost missed my curfew."

"I'm so sorry, Ella. You're right. I should've waited, but I didn't think it would take that long. I just needed to be there for her."

He steps forward, but I back up. This isn't good enough for me.

"Nate, I need to go to bed. I'm so tired. I'm not sure I can have this conversation right now."

He stands there. He doesn't move or speak.

"We can talk about it tomorrow, okay?" I say.

"You'll still be talking to me?"

"Yes, I'll still be talking to you."

"I'll call you."

I nod my head and try to look as sincere as possible, then I quietly shut the door and stand for a minute, taking deep breaths. I go upstairs slow and steady, but in my room under the covers, I start to let go. I cry into the pillow, mourning the things I miss from my old life: the city in spring, our old house with my room under the eaves, my friends, and my big sisters, especially Beck, who could really come through in a crisis like this.

And just before my exhaustion turns toward sleep, I remember all the things I would've missed if I hadn't moved here: my first hit, my first date, my first fat lip, my first prom. I wouldn't know Nate, and I wouldn't be lying here missing the chance to have our first kiss.

Championships

Chapter 37

The phone rings off the hook all day. First Christine, Jen, and Amy call and put me on speaker. They're laughing and yelling questions at me.

"One at a time," I say.

"Okay, did you kiss him with your fat lip?" Christine demands.

I don't have the energy to tell them the truth. I whisper, "Yes," which must come out really loud on the other end because they start clapping and whistling.

"How was it?"

"Awkward, but nice." I wish.

They seem satisfied. They're about to take the El to a street fair in Old Town. I feel that familiar pang and imagine going with them. There are always a hundred things going on in the city in the spring.

Later Frannie calls. "How's your lip?"

"Better."

"And the big prom?"

I still can't bring myself to talk about it, especially since I haven't heard from Nate. "I'll tell you guys all about it tomorrow. I gotta go. My dad wants me to help him work in the yard, and I have to start my protest."

In the afternoon, when I'm in the garden with my father (having lost the battle), my mother comes out with the phone for me.

I wipe my hands, tuck the phone under my chin. "Hello?"

"Ella, it's me, Nate."

"Hi." I turn away from my parents and go into the house.

"How are you? Are you okay? Did you sleep all right?" He's nervous and for some reason this irritates me.

"I slept fine."

There's a silence I don't know how to fill. I don't even know if I want to.

"I just wanted to tell you again how sorry I am about last night," Nate says. "I never meant to . . . ruin everything. I'd come over and talk to you in person, but there's stuff going on here at home. I can't leave."

"Sure. I'm busy, anyway. So, I'll see you tomorrow."

I hang up and set the phone in my lap, inspect my dirty hands and fingernails. How will things be tomorrow at school?

The phone rings, right there on my thigh, and I pick it up, thinking it might be Nate calling back, but it's Rocky.

"Hey," she says. "Anthony told me about last night. You okay?"

"Yeah, he really came through for me."

"That's Anthony, Super Cop. In his dreams. How's the lip?"

"Fine. Nate came by last night, later. To apologize."

"It was about Sally, wasn't it?"

I'm not surprised that she guessed this. "Yeah, it was."

"You know she must've planned it, right? I bet she did it on purpose."

"Probably," I say. "Anyway, let's drop it for a while. How are *you*?"

"I've been better," she says quietly.

My stomach plummets. "What's wrong?"

"Well, I have four days to convince my dad that being in Tulsa, Oklahoma, for the finals won't destroy the family."

"I thought he was over that. He knows how important this is to you!"

"He fell apart on Saturday, according to Anthony. He thought my not being around threw everybody off. Thomas missed a baseball game. Mikey wouldn't go to swimming class. He cried the whole time. Theresa can't cook to save her life. I mean, I was gone for a total of, what, eight hours? Chaos. I don't know if he hasn't had enough time to get used to me not being around every second or if he actually needs me at home."

"Let's talk to Coach," I say.

After a minute of silence, Rocky says, "Let me think about it, okay, El?"

At school the next day, I don't talk about prom or Nate or going to the *Show Boat* dress rehearsal. The Rocky situation is urgent. I brief Frannie and Mo on the details. At lunch, we sit in wait for her, hardly talking or cracking jokes. I don't even look in the direction of Nate's table, and neither of them, thankfully, is in the mood to probe. Finally, Rocky comes up. She slides her tray across the table and shakes her head.

"It's all over."

"But what did he say? Can't we fix this?" I plead.

"Ella, it's over." Rocky looks down at her untouched lunch and gets up. "I can't eat this."

As she cuts through the maze of cafeteria tables, Frannie says, "Go after her."

"No. I'm gonna go talk to Coach myself. She'll know what to do."

In the athletic office, Dixie and two of the guy coaches are hanging out. I ask, "Is Coach Lauer here?" and Coach pokes her head out of the AD's office. She comes out and says, "I've got first graders in five minutes. Wanna walk and talk, Ella?"

"Sure."

We walk to a shed by the gym, and she unlocks it. Inside is a mini equipment room with balls of every size and cones and bats and sticks and helmets.

"Wow," I say.

"I know. Don't you wish you had one of these growing up?"

I raise my eyebrows.

"There's nothing like the smell of grass and mud and sweat and mold to really get you going." She pulls out cones and red kick balls. "Listen, I talked to Rocky's father this morning."

"What can we do?"

Looking out across the playing field, she sighs.

"We can't play in the championships without her," I moan.

"Yes. We can. And we might have to. It's not up to me. And it's not up to you."

I'm so frustrated I'm afraid if I open my mouth I might start yelling.

"I know how you feel, but as much as I love this sport and this team, sometimes other things are more important," she says.

Which is not at all what I want to hear.

Behavioral Science is a bust. Nate watches me, but I can't even manage a smile. I don't know how to talk to him about prom or how to explain about Rocky. I can't seem to deal with anything at the moment. Thankfully he doesn't push the issue today, and I bolt as soon as class ends.

At practice, Rocky throws with me, but she does it without talking or even really looking at me. I can't figure out what's going on. Is she blaming me for getting her back on the team? Is it my fault for getting her hopes up, for making her think she deserves a life of her own?

After our first three drills we stop for water, and I notice that Sally isn't here. I haven't seen her all day, and I'm not sure if this has to do with my focus on Rocky or if she's actually absent. Coach stands with her back to the Peyton Plastics building, where there are no workers anywhere in sight. It makes it kind of lonely out here. Like we're practicing in a vacuum. I wonder if Coach and Mack Elliott are still an item.

"As most of you know, the conference divides the teams into two divisions at the championships. Depending on your record, you're placed in one of two brackets, and you only play the teams in your division."

I'm trying to listen hard and not look at Rocky or think about what must be going through her head.

"We're in Division II. Fort Worth Country Day is in Division I, ranked number one, so we won't be able to kick their butts this season. But we're seeded well in Division II, which means we play Oakridge again in the first game."

She holds up a stack of paper. "Here's your homework assignment. Sue Bee collected statistics from the other teams in our division from our games against them this season and last. Take them home and study them. Memorize the names, numbers, positions, and batting profiles. Look at their records against other teams in our bracket. Learn as much as you can. This kind of preparation will only make us better competitors."

I can't help but look at Rocky now. This is right up her alley. She loves analyzing data.

But she's staring into space.

A bad sign. It makes me think Rocky is throwing in the towel.

Chapter 38

On the way home, Theresa asks a million questions about prom, about who was wearing what and where we went to eat. Anthony obviously didn't share my sob story with everyone in the family. I answer questions, but mostly I look over at Rocky and get no response from her.

In my driveway I say, "Call me if you want to talk, okay?"

Rocky nods, giving me a closed-mouth smile so fake I want to scream.

After dinner, I do the dishes while my mother talks wedding plans on the phone with my sister Liz. Only two months to go. I slip off to my room to study my stats packet. My father appears at the doorway.

"Everything going all right at school?" he asks. No softball analogies in sight.

"Yeah." I turn around in my desk chair to face him.

He's leaning against the door frame.

"Everything okay at work?" I say, trying to keep things moving.

"Oh, sure. Just wanted to know you're keeping up with your studies as well as your baseball."

"Softball, Dad. With girls, it's called softball."

"Right." He nods.

As he backs away, I say, "Dad, I need some advice."

He grimaces as if this might hurt.

"It's not bad," I say. "It's about Rocky and her dad. She doesn't think he's gonna let her go to Tulsa for the championships."

He comes into my room and sits on the bed. "Because she'll be away too long?"

"Yeah. He thinks everything falls apart when she's gone. I don't think it's fair. She never gets to do anything for herself."

"You're right. It's not fair."

"What can I do?"

He swallows. "I'm not sure you can do anything, Ellie."

"But, Dad. She's my friend."

We look at each other for a minute. "Sometimes things like this have a way of working themselves out," he says. "Give it time."

Later, as I lie in bed, I know we don't have time. I need to come up with something fast.

Finally, during Spanish the next day, a plan begins to materialize in my head. I need to talk to Rocky before practice, if possible, but I don't see her. I see Nate, coming toward me from across the quad.

"Ella Kessler," he says. "You're avoiding me." He smiles, looking nervous.

I can't help but smile back, finally. "Not intentionally." I explain about Rocky.

I want to say more, maybe ask his advice, but I've decided not to tell anyone extra about my plan. Not Frannie and Mo, not my parents. Not even Rocky. To make it work, it has to be executed in secrecy. In the dead of night. And besides, I'm still not sure how I feel about Nate.

"So, I'll see you in class?" he says.

"Of course."

At practice, I try to be upbeat. I try to make jokes like Frannie and throw a little physical comedy into the mix. But Coach isn't having any of it.

"Ella, if you can't keep it together, why don't you take a few laps around campus?"

"Sorry, Coach. I'm okay. Better than okay."

In the locker room, Rocky tells me, "I can practice with the team this week, but I need to be home this weekend. Tulsa is officially off."

I nod my head. I don't bother asking questions. It's time for action. It's time to talk to Theresa.

Chapter 39

By Thursday I've got my instructions with backup plans typed and tucked in an envelope. I sneak them into Theresa's cubby after third period, and the next time I see her, she gives me the slightest nod. My perfect partner in crime: discreet, aloof, and reckless enough to want an adventure, any adventure. Plus, she's still so enamored by the fact that I actually went to prom she'd do anything for me. And really, she'd do anything for Rocky, she just won't admit it.

I have a plan worked out for Nate, too. I'm going to talk to him enthusiastically about nothing during Behavioral Science. I'm going to be friendly and interested and look him right in the eye. Surely I can just plow through this thing. But he's not there. He's excused for dress rehearsals and the plan falls flat.

Practice is bittersweet. My first season of playing a sport is over. I feel so different. Stronger. And smarter about something I hardly knew anything about before. Girls who were strangers are now friends, not the kind who hang out at your cubby between classes, but the kind who high-five you on the field when you make a good play; there's something deeper about that. For Kat and Marcie, the team's two seniors and co-captains, it's the last practice of their high school careers. They give emotional speeches about never forgetting us and hoping we make Division I next year. Frannie performs a little song and dance that she made up, and Coach praises them for their leadership. And then that part is over, too.

Coach quizzes us on the stats for Friday's first game—we've got 'em down cold—and informs us what time to be at the bus tomorrow morning. She collects permission slips but doesn't read a lineup. She barks out some orders for drills, but none of us breaks a sweat. Sally is present, but detached during practice. I try, but I can't muster any sympathy for whatever she went through at prom, real or imagined.

I haven't decided whether I'm going to Nate's dress rehearsal for *Show Boat*. He only mentioned it that once. But after practice, Frannie and Mo want to know if I'm going and I say yes without a moment's hesitation.

The car ride home takes forever. We're all quiet. Theresa and I exchange a look, I think. She's so understated I can't be sure.

At drop-off, I say, "Hang in there, Rock."

Theresa gets out of the car to take my seat in front. She rolls her lips together to keep from smiling. She seems to have more confidence in my plan than I do.

At the front door, my mother greets me, drying her hands on her apron. "Maureen called. She wants to know if you need a ride to the dress rehearsal."

I know what's coming.

"You didn't tell me Nate was the lead in *Show Boat*."

I don't have time to say anything before she gushes, "Daddy's working late, and I love *Show Boat*, you know that. I'd love to see him perform."

I say, "Mother, you can't go." I can't let her think everything's fine and dandy with Nate.

"I won't sit with you girls. You won't even know I'm there."

"Mom, no, I'm sorry."

She looks so hurt, I want to explain or at least try to make her feel better, but I don't. Instead, I call Mo back. She'll pick me and Frannie up around seven. I shower, eat, and cram in some studying before she arrives, avoiding my mom as much as possible.

We sit near the back of the auditorium. I can see Sally, Gwen, and Joy in front.

From the moment the curtain rises, you can tell that Nate's having so much fun. He's in his element, and I have this flash to the future, reading *People* magazine, where they show a picture of him from his high school production of *Show Boat* and now he's some big movie star. In every scene, even if someone else is singing, you can't take your eyes off him. It's a good thing he's the lead. If he weren't, he'd steal the show.

I'm nearly crying at the end because he's so good. I don't know how I can possibly deal with my feelings for him, my contempt for his sister, and my plan for Rocky all in one night. So I let it go for now. I'll give it time, like my father said.

After the stage goes dark, Mo says, "You going backstage to congratulate him?"

"I was thinking about it."

"Are you kidding? You have to," Frannie says.

"Will you guys come with me?"

"Absolutely," they say together.

We start down the row that leads to the backstage door when, out of nowhere, Sally, Gwen, and Joy come and block our way. I can tell something's very wrong because of the way Gwen and Joy look at me, and how Sally's eyes fix on mine.

"You're not going backstage to see Nate, are you?" Sally says.

"It was a great show, wasn't it?" Frannie says to Gwen and Joy.

Sally glares at her, then to me, "Isn't this thing over yet?"

"What thing?" I ask, my voice bland, but I can feel that she's about to blow. And no explanation can change the fact that she's *mean*. And although it may not be *about* me, I'm still in the crosshairs.

"The *thing* with my brother."

I try to find it in my heart to forgive her. For everything. But I feel nothing. Which doesn't mean I've found something fantastic to say back to her. So once again, I'm speechless.

"Well, that answers that, doesn't it?" She steps back and points toward the exit to the lobby. "I think you meant to go that way."

Frannie, Mo, and I file past them and out into the lobby, which is still crammed with people. I can hardly look at them. "God," I hiss. "I'm so pathetic. I can't . . . do anything."

"You're not the only one," Frannie says. "She likes to catch her prey unaware. It never fails."

"Should we go get something to eat?" Mo offers.

"No, I've got a paper due for English tomorrow that I have to finish," I say.

And they both nod their understanding. I appreciate the quiet on the ride home, and when I get out, Mo says, "Try to get some sleep, Ella. Big day tomorrow."

Inside, a note on the kitchen table reads: *Alarm set for 6. Hope you had a good time. Dad*

Mom's still mad about the play, otherwise she would've left the note.

I wish I could disappear for one week, so I wouldn't have to deal with Sally in Tulsa, where who knows what might happen. I wouldn't have to worry about whether Rocky will show up tomorrow or get in trouble with her dad. Maybe I should look for summer jobs in Chicago since I have to be up there for the wedding, anyway. I could stay with Christine and hide from everything bad in my life. Go back to who I used to be.

Chapter 40

The bus leaves at seven sharp. I hug my father good-bye and get in the car with my mom, who is still acting a little cool with me. I'm nervous and tired, and I want to tell her everything, that I've done something that might get me and Rocky and Coach in trouble. By now, Theresa will have packed a bag for Rocky, arranged pickup after school with their aunt Rita, and appointed Anthony ringmaster to get everyone off to school this morning early, so that Rocky makes it to the bus on time.

"If you forgot to pack anything," my mother says, "call me, and Dad and I will bring it up when we come."

"Thanks, Mom."

"We'll be up by this afternoon's game, okay?"

I lean over and give her a kiss on the cheek, and she smiles, but not too big.

I slip my overnight bag over my shoulder and get out of the car. I drop off my paper at the English Department then head to the gym. There are lots of athletes roaming around, since the track and tennis teams are also riding with us to the championships. Almost everyone is fresh out of the shower and looking a little rough around the edges. Frannie and Mo are helping

Coach stow bags under the bus and I glance around casually, first for Rocky, then for Sally. No sign of either yet.

Whether Rocky shows or not, I decide to explain everything to Frannie and Mo once we get on the bus.

Coach calls to Sue Bee, who looks like she's been up for hours. "How many are we missing?"

And then a car pulls up in the parking lot, Anthony's shiny green Honda. Rocky's in the passenger's seat, looking right at me. Mo's saying something to me, but I can't hear. I can't believe Rocky made it.

Anthony gets out at the same time as Rocky. Everyone stops talking and turns to stare at him. Coach says, "Who's that?" and then she sees Rocky.

I walk over to the car a few steps behind Coach. She hugs Rocky and says something to Anthony over the hood of the car. Theresa gets out of the backseat and helps the little boys. She grins at me, and I give her a thumbs up.

"Yeah, and now we're at school an hour early," she says, but she's smiling.

Rocky gives her an awkward hug, then kisses her younger brothers. "Be good," she says.

"You, too," Mikey says earnestly.

To me, Rocky says in her quietest voice, "Thank you."

"How could we do it without you?" I say before the rest of the team crowds around us.

Coach gives me a scolding look but can't hide the gratitude in her eyes. "We'll talk about this later," she says.

We find seats in the back of the bus. I have a perfect view of the aisle when Sally climbs aboard. I pretend to be fully engrossed in a conversation with my friends. It shouldn't be like this, but it is. Sally's stuck sitting up front. And I've narrowly escaped another scene with her.

When Coach, Dixie, Sue Bee, and the tennis coach, Miss Sommers, confirm that everyone who should be on the bus is on the bus, the driver pulls out. Next to me at the window, Rocky waves to her family. Anthony, Theresa, and the little boys stand around the shiny green car, watching us. But this is a huge bus with tinted windows, so they can't see her. Rocky stands up and knocks on the window, presses her palms against the pane.

"Hey!" she yells. There's so much noise on the bus that no one can hear the sadness in her voice except me.

She sits down. "They know how much you love them," I tell her.

"Yeah." Rocky glances at me. "Thanks for having something up your sleeve."

"Theresa was the one who did everything."

"She really came through. But listen. I have to tell you something. He doesn't know."

I have this weird feeling she's talking about Nate. "Know what?" I ask tentatively.

"He doesn't know I'm here."

"Your father?"

She nods.

"You didn't tell him?"

"I couldn't. I couldn't do it. I know it was part of the plan, but I couldn't do it. Theresa and Anthony are gonna try to explain, and then I'll just deal with the consequences when we get back."

I lean my head against the padded seat and close my eyes. All I can think is, *Oh no.*

Chapter 41

Rocky gives a shrug, and tells me she doesn't want to talk about it anymore. She asks me if I went to Nate's dress rehearsal, and I give her the same shrug.

"What happened?"

"Sally accosted me in front of Frannie and Mo. So I didn't go backstage. He didn't even know I was there."

"*What?*" Rocky leans forward in her seat. "You didn't laugh in her face?"

Frannie and Mo pop up over the seats. "What're we missing?" Frannie asks.

"Nothing," I say before Rocky gets a chance.

Frannie looks at Mo. "Do you ever get that feeling there's a lot going on here we don't know anything about?"

I throw a wadded-up gum wrapper at Frannie, and she ducks. "See what I mean?" she yells from her hiding place behind the seat.

Dixie's voice interrupts us. She holds up a letter in one hand. "Ladies, ladies. I need your attention for one minute."

There's still music, laughter, and some talking, but she's got as much quiet as she's gonna get.

"I have a letter here from Mr. Michaels, our beloved headmaster. I'm required to read it to you before we arrive in Tulsa. And since we're still intact one minute away from campus, I figure now is as good a time as any. He says, 'Sports teams: Congratulations and best of luck in the SPC tournament this weekend. Although the thrill of competition is exciting and rewarding in many ways, remember you are representing Spring Valley Day School on and off the playing fields. Please respect your coaches and chaperones.' *That means us*," Dixie says. "And then he ends with: 'We are proud to have you as ambassadors of our fine school. Sincerely,' and so on."

We all start laughing and cheering. Apparently everyone thinks the headmaster's a geek. I've never even met the guy. The minute Dixie stops talking, everyone resumes their level of noise.

I lean over to Rocky and say, "I don't want to talk about the Sally thing. You don't want to talk about your dad. Call it even?"

She nods. And so we talk about softball.

Rocky says, "This whole week I've been having softball dreams, and they're so real. Like normal games. Everyone's in uniform. The ball is one of the new, white game balls. We play well: three up, three down. We're high-fiving each other. The stands are full. Mr. Zawicki is there. Did I ever tell you about Mr. Zawicki?"

I shake my head, but I'm caught up thinking how I love being on this bus with all these girls who play sports, even if Sally Fontineau, who wants to ruin my life, is half a bus in front of me. I love how brave Rocky is to be here on her way to Tulsa. I love that I'm on a team. I can hardly remember when I wasn't. It's not like every girl is my best friend. I don't even know everyone that well. It's just a thing that I feel a part of. It makes everything different.

Rocky's still talking. "He was my gym teacher the first time I ever played softball. He pulled me aside after class and said, 'Miss

O'Hara, that's very impressive.' And I said, 'What is?' And he said, 'Your arm.' So I looked at my arm because I was little, and I didn't know that an impressive arm meant a good throw."

I try to imagine the scenario and it makes me smile.

"Yeah, he laughed at that, too, in a really nice way. He told me, 'You don't throw like a girl, Miss O'Hara. And this is a very good thing.'

"I had no idea what he was saying, but I understood that throwing a ball got me noticed. It was kind of a big moment for me." She shrugs. "Not that I agree with the girl part. I think I throw exactly like a girl should. But in that moment when I figured out I could throw a ball, it was like I understood the world better. And the world understood me."

"I *knew* you were the one to teach me to throw like a girl."

I've never been good enough at anything to feel like I understand the world. But Rocky's story makes me feel a little better. As if I'm helping her fulfill something that she was meant to do all along. Won't her father have to understand that?

The hotel in Tulsa is about a hundred stories high and has a fountain in the lobby and a pool off the main hallway that you can see through glass windows. Everyone from our bus is on the tenth floor. It's like a sorority, with our bags and pillows and good-luck teddy bears. Doors slam, music blares. It's magnificent. We check out the rooms—ours has a great view of Tulsa, which is nothing like Chicago or Dallas, but it's cool to be up high enough to see the whole downtown.

I hope my parents don't end up on this floor.

From the hallway we hear Coach yelling into a bullhorn that we have to be down for lunch in our uniforms in fifteen minutes.

That gets us screaming and bustling.

After pooling our snacks together and choosing the ones we want to bring to our first game (sunflower seeds and Starbursts), we dress in full uniform. Frannie demands that we check the comfort quotient of the mattresses before heading down to lunch. So we jump around for her benefit. Of course, she tries to flip from one bed to the next, hits the lamp with her foot, nearly breaks her neck falling to the floor, and ends up with the lamp in her lap.

We hold our breath until Frannie says, "I think that's the best catch I ever made."

From the lobby we're ushered into a large room with lines of tables, not unlike the school cafeteria. On each table is a box with bag lunches.

"Don't worry, they're provided by the hotel," Dixie says.

I'm so excited about our game, about being here and not in school, that I'm starved and nauseous at the same time. All I can manage to eat is a slightly green banana.

At the host school, Holland Hall, the playing fields and track and tennis courts are teeming with kids and coaches. It's wild to think that everyone here is missing school. Everyone will participate in something competitive—a race, a match, a game. Back at my old school, we had a really good basketball team that always went to state. I just had no idea what it meant. And now here I am.

Before I know it, we're on the field warming up. Frannie says she spotted my parents wandering around.

"I saw the scarf."

"Oh, no!"

"Is it unlucky today? Or lucky?" Mo says.

"I can't remember!"

Rocky's throwing so hard that my hand stings.

I yell, "Zawicki sure knew what he was talking about."

She cracks a smile.

Coach blows her whistle and gathers us under a tree. It's so hot the ground is like a furnace pumping heat up through our cleats.

"Drink a lot of water and keep your hats on." She passes water bottles around. "I know this is so much fun. It's fun for me, too. And we're going to have tons of adventures before we get home, but I need for y'all to get your heads in this game . . . right now. We barely beat Oakridge the last time. They're gonna want this game. Be ready for that."

She claps her hands, then says, all passionate and serious, "Get your game face on and make this *ours* from the first pitch. Own it. And remember, you've got to want it more."

We start cheering, then stand up, clapping and hollering. The umps call the captains to home plate. We lose the toss, which means we're away, which means we're at bat first. And that's it. Gwen's standing in the batter's box: *The game has begun.*

I spy my parents in the stands, and my mom gives me a private wave, trying not to do anything that would embarrass me. I wish I could run over there and apologize for being moody and thank her for being such a steady fan, scarf and all.

Gwen gets a hit, a nice poke between first and second, and she's easily safe. Virginia pops out, holding Gwen at first, and Kat gets a single to left field. With runners on first and second, Rocky's in the batter's box, and it's time for me to get up casually, find my bat, swing it a bit, then watch Rocky blast a one-hop double between second and third. She sends Gwen and Kat home and makes it safely to second.

Oh, the pressure. With one out, ahead by two, I get up to bat, don't look at my parents, and try to decipher Coach's sign: four fingers brush over her right eyebrow. Wait on it.

I'm never patient enough to wait on pitches, even when they're obvious balls. But today I am. Today I'm in the box with a confident stance and a lucky bat. I remember this pitcher from our last game against Oakridge, and I hit off her by waiting it out. So I do just as Coach says.

Now the count is suddenly 3 and 0. She throws me a strike, but I expected it. I'm 3 and 1. I step out of the box calmly. My best friend has one foot against second base and the other stretching out in front of her. She's poised to run. She knows I can do this.

The next pitch drifts over the plate like it's floating, like it's in slow motion. I twitch my right arm up and back a bit and then swing hard. The ball connects a few inches from the end of my bat—the middle of the sweet spot—and sails between right and center field. Both fielders are going after it as I round first. I slide into second as Rocky crosses home plate. We're up 3–0 in the very first inning!

My parents cheer in the bleachers. Everyone on the bench high-fives Rocky. Coach jumps up and down by the third-base line. And I see Sally Fontineau chitchatting with one of the ninth graders as if she couldn't care less.

It occurs to me, as I stand on second base, the sun pounding down on my batting helmet, that Sally is inconsequential to my life. I'll figure things out with Nate. I'll take finals. I'll find a summer job here in Dallas. I'll start school in the fall. And I'll answer back the next time Sally tries to harass me. I'll start standing up for myself off the field, the same way I do on it. Because there's no reason in the world why I shouldn't.

It's like that moment when Rocky discovered that softball made her world clearer. I think it's making mine clearer, too.

We beat Oakridge 5 to 0. We're on our way.

In the huddle after the game, Coach says, "That was good. No, that was great. You played well. You got off to a quick start offensively and played flawless defense." She looks around at all of us. "Way to go."

We cheer for ourselves because we're psyched.

"All right. You have a few choices for the rest of the afternoon. You may go and watch the end of the Episcopal game; they're on field four. Or you can go watch track or tennis or baseball. As long as you're back on that bus by five forty-five. And we meet in the lobby for dinner at seven. Got it?"

"Only an hour to get ready?" someone says.

And everyone laughs.

We all head in different directions. Rocky wants to watch the end of the Episcopal game. Before we take off I tell the girls I have to go see my parents. They're standing by the bleachers. The four of us walk over together, and my mom tries to tone it down, but can't help hugging each of us. No one seems to mind.

"What a game," she keeps saying.

My father says, "I'm so proud of you, Ellie."

We say our good-byes and walk toward the other softball field. I think about telling the girls about my little epiphany on second base.

But then I decide to keep it to myself. For now.

Chapter 42

Back at the hotel, we take turns in the shower until the whole room steams up. Towels and brushes and dirty uniforms are everywhere. Mo orders us to get the room halfway organized and at least hang our uniforms in the closet for tomorrow's games. She dresses in a clean pair of khakis and a red shirt. Her blond hair, combed back off her face, falls right into place even though it's wet.

Frannie sees this and says to Mo, "Is it hard being you?"

With Frannie, everything's a joke: her flaming red hair, her freckles, her full figure. Life rolls off her pretty easily.

As the youngest of four girls, I know about waiting for the bathroom and fighting to get mirror space.

Pacing around the room in her towel, Rocky seems out of place. After a while, she says, "I have nothing to wear. Theresa didn't pack me anything for going out to dinner."

That gets us started trading things. First she tries on Mo's red shirt, since Mo naturally brought several different outfits.

But the red doesn't suit Rocky, so Frannie says to me, "What's in your bag?"

"Jeans and two shirts." I take one, my sister Becky's. It's a white T-shirt with a light blue ribbon threaded around the collar.

I hand it to Rocky and she looks at me.

"Are you sure?"

"Yeah. Go ahead. My other one is a black peasant shirt."

"I wish *that* one fit me," Frannie says. "You've got more style than I thought."

Rocky pulls on the white shirt and says, "Oh, I like this a lot."

"It looks good," I say. Frannie and Mo nod in agreement.

With wardrobe completed, we work on drying our hair, tying our shoes, and making sure we have money for dinner and our keys to the room. Then we're off.

At the elevator we run into some tennis players decked out in their finest party wear: short skirts, skimpy tops, dangly earrings, makeup.

A few of them talk to Frannie and Mo as Rocky and I hang back. When the elevator arrives, it's nearly full, and since we can't all fit, Frannie encourages them to go ahead and we'll catch the next one.

"*Please*," Frannie says when the doors close. "Let's not go to dinner where the tennis team goes. They're too beautiful. It's intimidating."

In the lobby, it's more of the same. Even the track team looks dressed up.

"Are we underdressed?" Mo whispers.

And Frannie snaps back, "*I'm* not."

The coaches hand us our food allowance and tell us we have four choices for dinner outside of the hotel, with chaperones at each. Most of the baseball team lines up to go to the Beef Palace. The holy trinity are hop-skipping it over that way. After a quick consensus, we join the small group for the Black-Eyed Pea, with Coach and Dixie chaperoning.

From our booth in the back, we happen to be in *the* prime

location to see Mack Elliot walk in the door. I nudge Mo, who's also facing that way, and then Rocky and Frannie turn around to see. He's wearing jeans and a white button-down shirt. He stands at Coach's table for a minute, obviously pleased that he's surprised her, while she stumbles trying to get up to greet him. We're all groaning at the missteps. He goes to give her a kiss on the cheek but she fouls that up, too, turning her head too far so he misses the mark.

We can't stop giggling.

"Oh. My. God. She's totally in love with him," Mo says, taking the words right out of my mouth.

We can't stop watching Coach, Mack, and Dixie. They seem to be in a heated discussion and we make guesses about the topic. By eight thirty, after we've split three different desserts, we decide it's time to leave since Coach gave us a ten o'clock curfew and we want to hit the hotel game room before then.

Back at the lobby, we gaze into the crowded room filled with pinball machines, a Ping-Pong table, a pool table, foosball, and two small bowling alleys. It's crawling with kids our age.

Rocky's not into it. "I need to call home," she says to me. "Tell them I've gone up."

"Good luck," I say.

After she disappears I see that Mo and Frannie have gone off to be social, and I'm stuck sitting on a grubby stool watching all the people, thinking about Nate, and wishing I could call him, but I don't have the nerve. The confidence thing hasn't quite made its way into the boy arena.

A few guys I don't know start to play pinball near me. They're keyed up and talking loud. One of them notices me and asks, "Who are you?"

"I'm Ella." I don't recognize them from Spring Valley.

"You don't look like you're having much fun, Ella."

I stand and push back my stool. "Oh, no. I'm good," I say.

"I bet," another guy says.

I think that might be an insult, but I'm not sure.

I look around for Mo and Frannie. But instead, I see Sally, staring right at me, raising her eyebrows, shaking her head slowly. As if to imply I'm flirting with these boys or something.

I don't know who I hate more: these obnoxious boys or Sally. But I step away from the guys and walk toward Sally. I think the time is right to deal with it.

It must surprise her, the way the distance between us lessens. Suddenly I'm in her face.

"Enjoying yourself?" Sally asks.

"I came to find out what that look was all about."

"What look?"

"The one you gave me from across the room."

She shrugs, completely uninterested in our conversation.

But I refuse to be dismissed anymore.

"Sally, I want to tell you that I think it was completely wrong of you to forbid me to see Nate last night. You don't own him."

"Neither do you. And, by the way, he never asked where you were or anything."

I feel a momentary punch in the gut. "That's not the point," I say. "I don't know what your problem is with me. And I don't even care. I just want you to know that I'm done with you walking all over me. Nate might feel bad for you, but I don't. You're pathetic. You don't want anyone else to be happy, because you're not. Don't you ever want to be less mean?"

She doesn't respond.

"Anyway, we only have one more day of softball and then

we're no longer teammates, not that you ever acted like one. But at least I won't have to look at you every day and wonder why anyone would want to be friends with you."

I don't wait for her reaction. I turn and walk to the elevators by myself, push number ten, and squeeze my eyes closed. It wasn't grand. It didn't even feel that good, but it was a start.

In the room, Rocky's watching TV. "Where're Bert and Ernie?" she says.

"Still down there. How'd it go?"

She shakes her head. "I couldn't do it. I don't want to ruin this moment. This is so fun and so pure. I'll talk to him when I get home. I can't worry about it now."

"You can have that shirt if you want. It looks good on you."

She laughs. "Oh, Ella."

"So, I've got some news. I went up to Sally."

"You did? What did you say?"

"I said, you better lay off or Rocky's gonna beat you up."

She howls with laughter. "Did you really?"

"*No.*" I tell her what actually happened.

Rocky studies me. "And you think that's bad? Compared to all the things she's said and done to you, that's nothing."

"It didn't feel like nothing."

"Well, don't lose sleep over it. *She* won't."

"Right."

Mo and Frannie barge in, laughing hysterically.

"I wish we had a Ping-Pong team at school." Frannie giggles. "I would be so popular!"

We're ready for bed when the knock on the door comes at ten fifteen.

"You're my last room," Coach says from the hallway.

Frannie opens the door and says, "Because we're your favorites?"

Coach just smiles. "Don't stay up all night watching TV and eating junk food."

"Hey, Coach, what happened with your cute construction guy?" Mo asks.

I swear Coach blushes. "Oh, nothing."

"He was up here on work?" Frannie asks, even though we know he wasn't.

"Something like that. All right, y'all. Lights out in fifteen minutes. Okay?"

We stay up late watching HBO and talking about Coach, Mack Elliot, and what fun it is to sleep in a hotel. Later, I lie in the dark listening as everyone's breathing drops deeper into sleep. Finally, my brain still unable to shut down, I get up and sit at the window, watching the lights of Tulsa. No matter what happens tomorrow, I decide it'll be a good day.

Chapter 43

In the morning we're groggy but excited. We throw on our uniforms, and carry the bags with our gloves, caps, water bottles, and sunscreen.

"I'm having French toast," Frannie says as we get on the elevator. "My mother never makes me that."

We walk through the lobby into the conference room, which is Spring Valley's makeshift dining room for the weekend. There's a long buffet with rows of steaming breakfast food: French toast, waffles, pancakes, eggs, bacon, sausage links, sausage patties, biscuits, gravy, hash browns, and oatmeal. At the far end of the buffet is everything else: fruit, cereals, juice, milk, bagels, muffins, and croissants. The athletes and coaches walk around with heaping plates like they're hypnotized by the amount of food. Frannie is speechless.

"I'm starved," I say.

And we dig in.

After nine, everyone starts clearing their trays and slurping down their last bits of orange juice. Sally, Gwen, and Joy come in. Coach gets up and tells them to take something for the road because we're getting on the bus. Sally doesn't look at me, but I keep my eye on her.

From the bus I watch huge, beautiful clouds coming in from the west. I thought only Texas had these long, low lines of clouds that go on forever. But apparently Oklahoma has them, too. Only these clouds are different, because by the time we arrive at the school, the sky has darkened, and when we begin batting practice, it turns a solid green-purple stretching from the horizon to just above the treetops. This must be some kind of sign.

The umpires look worried and say to Coach, "Let's see how many innings we can play before it hits."

But she tells us in the huddle, "It's not gonna rain. That's how positive thinking works, okay?" She looks around at us. "I mean it. We win this game, we're in the finals."

"All right!" we yell.

My stomach's in knots, as usual.

Coach says, "Last night I couldn't sleep."

Join the club.

"So I got up and wrote a little pep talk. But you know what? You don't need a pep talk. You don't need *me* to tell you how to play the game anymore. You *know* how to play the game. Now it's just time to show everyone else."

We stomp our feet and yelp and whistle.

The game starts as quickly as yesterday's. First we're warming up, next we're at bat. Playing the school hosting the tournament puts any team at a disadvantage: Their fans pack the bleachers, the team knows their field by heart, they slept in their own beds, in their own rooms. By the end of the second inning, Holland Hall has jumped ahead by two runs. They keep their roll alive in the top of the third by picking off Kat when she tries to steal second.

But then Rocky's up to bat. She never ceases to amaze me. With everything going on in her head, she's still so cool in the batter's box. So tough looking. As if she'll crush the ball to bits. I'd be terrified if I were the pitcher.

Rocky glances at Coach, waits for the signs. Coach claps her hands. "Okay, batter. Nice and easy. Nothing flashy."

And Rocky nods her head.

She waits on the first two pitches and then a ball comes in, low and inside. I watch Rocky's knees drop a bit. She's gonna swing. She's gonna pulverize that ball. And she does, with everything, her whole body. Nothing "nice" about it. There's that perfect, high *ping* sound and the ball flies so far over the left fielder's head that she drops her glove and takes off after it. Rocky's long, strong legs soar around the bases. Her rhythm is exactly even, and she doesn't stutter before touching first, then second and third. She crosses home plate, and we run to congratulate her as the rain begins to fall lightly.

She says to Coach, "Sorry about that. The pitch was too round. My favorite kind. I had to swing away."

"Sure," Coach says, smiling.

But the rest of the game continues to go something like that. When Coach gives us signals to swing away, we hold back. When she tells us to stay on a base, we take the turn and safely launch ourselves headfirst into second or third or home plate. We do everything opposite of what she says, and it works.

We win 6 to 2. The rain holds off for most of the game but it starts to really pour as we drag the last of our equipment into one of the smaller gyms by the athletic fields.

"That felt good," Rocky says.

"Yeah." I search for the right words. "You were unbelievable."

She looks down. We're still wearing our cleats, on the threshold of the gymnasium, half in, half out.

She says, "I played like I might not ever play again." And then, gazing at me, she adds, "If you know what I mean."

The gyms are full of other athletes, so Coach leads us to a dim hallway and we set up camp, take off our cleats, wring out our socks, and pass around water bottles. Then Coach sits us down to have our postgame talk.

"What happens if we get rained out?" someone asks.

"I'm not sure," Coach says. "But it might be a good thing."

We wait for her to say more. I'm getting this feeling that even though we won, Coach isn't pleased.

"You played well out there," she says. "Confident, strong. But you played recklessly and that's dangerous. You stopped watching me and listening to me."

I catch Rocky's eye before her head goes down in shame.

"I'm proud that you're getting better and smarter, but don't get cocky. If you get too cocky, you start to overlook things and make mistakes. Trust me, it happens. And I'm not gonna let it happen to you. My prediction is that it's gonna stop raining and—"

A rumble of thunder interrupts her speech and breaks our straight, serious expressions.

"Okay, okay, I get the message. Enough scolding. We won. We're in the finals!" She punches her fist in the air.

And we follow her lead.

"Our game's at one thirty. Lunch,"—she pulls a soggy schedule from her bag—"is in the big gym, wherever that is."

One of the assistant baseball coaches from Spring Valley ducks his head into our dark hallway and says, "Coach, thought you'd want to know that Episcopal just beat St. Stephen's."

"Thanks, Rollie." She looks at us. "Well, now we know we're

playing Episcopal in the finals. I know some of you watched the end of that game yesterday. We'll talk a little strategy before infield. Until then, you're on your own."

By twelve thirty the rain has stopped and coaches help sweep water off the tennis courts and track. The maintenance crew dumps dry sand along the baselines of the softball field and fills puddles in the outfield. It'll be messy, but playable.

Before warm-up, Kat explains to us how playing in bad weather works to our advantage by evening out the teams.

Someone says, "You mean if it hadn't rained, we couldn't possibly win?"

Kat grins. "Not at all. I'm just saying we're really good at bad fields."

We laugh at this, joking about the Peyton Plastics building and our stubby field at home. Which makes us reminisce about our construction workers and Mack Elliot. Mo, Frannie, Rocky, and I exchange looks, but we don't say anything about seeing Mack last night with Coach. It doesn't sound like anyone else knows about it.

Before we leave for the field, I see my father wandering through the gym. He looks so out of place and old-fashioned. I wave. When he sees me, his whole face changes. He strides across the gym and gives me a big hug.

"What a day. Good game out there."

"Thanks. Where's Mom?"

"In the room."

"Everything's okay with her?"

"Sure. We just got back from lunch. We've made some new friends out here." He looks at me funny.

"Yeah, Dad. That's great. Well, wish us luck."

"Good luck," he says and walks with us as far as the gym door before he steps aside to let us through.

"Your dad's so cute," Mo says.

"For a dad," Frannie agrees.

And it feels like being with Christine, Jen, and Amy, who adore my dad.

We're on field four, which is the same field Episcopal played on yesterday when they won. A bad sign. Mo's rambling on about what we need to do to break the spell when Rocky stops so quickly in front of me that I bump right into her.

"Rock?"

Without looking at me, she reaches for my wrist and squeezes. And then I see where she's looking. In the bleachers: my mother, wearing what's now considered the lucky scarf again (except that she's wearing it on her head, which couldn't possibly be good), is blabbing to some woman I don't recognize. And there are kids beside her. And two men. And there's Anthony! And Theresa and Thomas and Mikey!

I say, "*Oh my God.*"

There in the stands, wearing Spring Valley caps and holding umbrellas, is Rocky's family. She points to the woman talking to my mother and says, "That's Aunt Rita, and Uncle Nick, and their kids."

"Is the other guy . . . ?"

She nods. "My father."

I hear my own gasp of surprise, as if it's coming from someone else.

"Did you do this, too?" she asks me suspiciously.

I shake my head. "No, really, I had no idea."

My father appears by the bleachers. Rocky's dad stands and gives him a hand to help him up.

Rocky and I stare at each other in disbelief.

"Did your parents do this?" she asks.

"They couldn't have. They didn't know about the plan."

Theresa sees us and waves, giving us her best reluctant smile.

"God," Rocky says. "Could Theresa . . . ?"

But we don't have time to figure it out. Coach is running infield and yelling at us to get in our positions. I watch Rocky trot to her spot between second and third. If she's scared, she's not showing it. It looks as if she's running on air.

Chapter 44

As the game starts, I'm hyperventilating—but I'm here, standing a few feet from first base, trying to act calm. The first two innings go scoreless. We're playing conservatively, maybe too conservatively, but we're nervous and Episcopal is good. Plus, Rocky hasn't gotten a ball yet, and I'm just waiting for something to happen so that her father can see her do something great.

By the bottom of the sixth, Rocky's been on base twice, both from walks, and there's still no score. But now, with one out, Episcopal has runners on first and third. It's a no-brainer. Their runner on first will steal second the minute Gwen pitches the ball. And even though Kat's got one of the best arms in the league, she won't throw it, because if she did, the runner on third would steal home.

Every one of us knows the game is about to change unless we can hold 'em. We've got to play smart. Let the runner get to second. We've got to play aggressive defense. Let the fielders make their plays. We've gotta have faith in one another. And then we've gotta kick butt at bat.

I look at Rocky. She nods at me, calls a heads up to Joy and Virginia. She yells, "Let's go, batter!"

The batter's sixth in the order and looks confident with

cocked wrists, her right elbow back and high. My heart races, using up all the blood in my legs, forcing me to dance around in the dirt, shaking out my feet and ankles.

Gwen sends a fastball over the plate. It's perfect. The ump calls a strike, and Kat leaps up from her squatting position and tears up the path toward the mound as if she might throw the ball. The runner beside me is too timid to move. Her coach yells at her. The count is 0 and 2. Rocky jogs onto the mound, gathering us there for a quick pep talk.

"She'll swing," Rocky barks.

"She won't," Gwen says.

"Be ready," Rocky says. "She'll swing."

And Rocky's right. When Gwen pitches another fastball, the batter takes a bite, but it's halfhearted, like she knew she wasn't supposed to. The ball spins off the bat, heading toward the gap between short and second. My runner has taken off, and the batter charges toward me. But Rocky's all over the ball, as if she willed it to come to her. She takes a few steps to her left, drops her glove to the dirt, snaps it around the ball, drags her foot over second base, and then hurls the ball to me. I stretch for it—my arm, my leg, my toes—and I catch it.

The umpire squats to watch the play, then leaps up to call the batter out.

"That's three, ladies," she yells, pulling a handkerchief from her back pocket and wiping her brow.

We turned two. Our favorite double play. We've gone through the motions a million times in practice, but never in a game has the throw from second been strong enough to make it to first before the runner, even when Rocky makes the play. I see her father stand up, clapping and smiling. He's so much smaller than I expected.

As we run off the field howling and cheering, we toss our gloves into a pile, trade caps for batting helmets, and slap each other on the backs. You'd think we'd won the game.

"You can do it," Coach keeps saying. "Base hits, base hits. One more inning. This is your . . ." And then she stops talking.

Frannie says, "You swallow a sunflower shell, Coach?"

But she still doesn't say anything.

Past the stands a group of families has gathered to cheer for us. My first thought is that they're at the wrong field, because I don't recognize them. I don't think anyone does, until the men put on their bright yellow hard hats. And Mack Elliot steps out from behind them.

Coach recovers. She waves and gives a slow nod to Mack. Everyone on the team is excited to see them—our very own cheerleaders. Even Sally Fontineau has an amused expression—not disgust for a change. There's hope.

We're at the bottom of the order—Joy, Debra, and Marcie—but Episcopal's pitcher is tired, and the balls come in erratically. Both Joy and Debra walk, and Marcie, with two ducks on the pond, hits a blooper over Short's head. It drops in the mud and stops dead, giving the runners time to get safely on their bags. The construction workers go crazy. These men with their wives and kids, using up their Saturday to come all the way up to Tulsa to root for a bunch of softball players they hardly even know.

Gwen's up. Lead-off batter. Bases loaded. No outs.

Her fly ball between left and center is caught dramatically with a slide through the mud and a crisscross of players. There's a big roar from our bench, but Episcopal gets the ball back to the pitcher before Joy, who isn't a confident base runner, can make a move off third base. One out. Coach signals to Virginia to go for a base hit. Nice and easy.

The pitch comes in clean and fast. Virginia smacks it into center field and brings Joy home without a problem. The fielder's quick, though, and she picks up the one-hopper and whips it to second for the second out, but we're on the scoreboard. *We're winning.*

With Virginia on first, Debra on third, and Kat in the box, Coach gives a little heads-up signal to the runners. We can't make the same mistake they did. The pitch comes in, Kat doesn't swing, Virginia takes off for second, and Debra takes a good, threatening lead off third. The catcher holds the ball, walks it to the pitcher.

It's picture perfect. We've got runners on second and third, two outs, and Kat hits an outside pitch to right field. The stands go wild. Debra runs for home. Virginia runs for third. But the right fielder makes an easy toss to first to put out Kat. And suddenly, we're at the bottom of the inning.

Rocky didn't get to bat. She's still standing in the on-deck circle with the bat in her hand. I know how much she wanted to hit that ball. To show her father what she's made of.

Coach goes over to her, leans in to whisper something, then pats her back. I love her for doing this. For knowing, despite everything else, that Rocky needed something extra.

Coach paces the sidelines. Claps her encouragement. Yells to us to hold them.

The inning goes by in a blur. I remember that Virginia made a blistering throw to me for the first out and that Kat caught a foul pop-up for number two. Now there's a runner standing next to me and another next to Rocky. How did that happen? What were the plays? Base hits? Did I get an error? Have I blacked out?

Don't let me fall apart. Let me be a part of winning. Please. I want this *one* thing.

The outcome of this game, of this season, seems to matter more than anything else has ever mattered to me, as if it's going to predict the outcome of my life.

I am certain that this is where I'm supposed to be. On this field. For this school. In this game. As crazy as all of it has been, I've made the pieces of my new life come together.

I hear Rocky call my name, and the batter whacks the ball about two feet to my left. The runner takes off behind me as the ball hurtles toward me. I have to backhand it, no question. I have to cross my arm in front of my face so that I can't even see. It happens in a split second.

In a blinding puff of dust, I snag the ball in the webbing of my glove and am so caught off balance it carries me to the ground. The runner has to leap over me, but I lift my glove to touch her, the ball still in my grasp. The ump calls the batter out.

Game over. We win!

Everyone is on their feet—my teammates on the field and on the bench, the parents, the construction workers. Rocky runs to help me up from the dirt. "You did it!" she screams. "You did it!"

I hand her the ball and she kisses it.

"*We* did it!" I scream back.

Those of us with family in the stands gravitate to them for hugs and congratulations. The others drift shyly, but gratefully, to the construction guys and their families. Mack Elliot handles introductions, and Rocky and I break away from our families to meet these other loyal fans. There's Hank and Charlie. Tom "Too-Tall" Marino. Jose H. and Jose R., Doug, Dave, Dan.

Another guy John-John. And Cesar. And Raymond, one of the only ones who didn't bring a wife and kids. They're just regular, friendly, helpful-looking guys.

Coach comes over. She says, "I know what a journey this has been for you." She shakes their hands. "Thank you for coming. It means the world to us." Finally she goes to Mack, takes his face in both her hands, and kisses him on the mouth. Everyone cheers.

Later, with the sky darkening, there's the presentation of the trophy—the smaller trophy, by the way (since the big one went to the Division I winners, Fort Worth Country Day). We stand at attention: grubby and sweaty and decorated with candy wrappers, silly sunglasses, colorful visors, strings of beads, and jangle bracelets. Coach stands beside us trying to act respectable, but I keep thinking of Mack's expression after the kiss, his surprise and delight. And it makes me think of Nate and how I wish he were here to see this.

The headmaster and athletic director from Holland Hall congratulate both teams and say a few words, but I'm hardly listening. Mr. Hardy, *our* athletic director, shows up late and joins the celebration. They hand the trophy over to Coach and she gives it to Kat and Marcie, the captains. They raise it above their heads and we pile in a big group hug, chanting, "*Chicks with mitts! Chicks with mitts!*" It's loud and damp and pretty fragrant here in the midst of the throng, but I love it because it smells like grass and mud and wet leather gloves. It smells like softball to me, and I can't believe I'm so lucky to know something like this. And something like winning.

Chapter 45

It's only been a day since we got to Tulsa, but the bus ride home feels a million times different than when we left. Like we share some big, beautiful secret. A lot of it comes from spending so much time with the same people: meals, warm-ups, games, curfews. And, of course, sharing a room with three of my new best friends. We hang over our seats and talk to everyone, even the tennis players and the sprinters and the long jumpers.

When we arrive back in Dallas, it's dark and parents are waiting and talking in the parking lot. I appreciate that my father is here, having made the trip back from Tulsa, and dropped off my mother, before coming back to school.

I say good-bye to everyone dramatically, as if we're parting for good.

My father says, "You must be beat."

And I realize that I am.

We have a quiet ride home, and as we pull in, my dad says, "I'd carry you to bed, but my back may not make it."

I smile. "I think I can get there on my own."

And that's the last I really remember.

On Sunday I sleep late and then walk around in a haze all day. I've got homework to catch up on and a phone call to Nate I should make, but can't yet. It feels like the one last missing piece to my happy puzzle.

I'm studying in my room when the doorbell rings. It's late afternoon, and I try to remember what day it is and who might be coming over.

"Ella, it's Nate," my father calls up the stairs.

My stomach flip-flops and I glance at my reflection.

As I come down the stairs, I see Nate's wearing shorts. I don't think I've ever seen him in shorts, and as I get closer I see his legs are hairy, like a man's, and that makes me even more nervous. I try to look away.

My father says, "Your mother and I are out back if you two need anything." And then he disappears, and it's just me and Nate in the dimness of the front hall.

"I hope this is okay, me coming over like this. Your dad didn't say anything, so. . . ."

"He doesn't know about prom."

"He doesn't?"

I shake my head. "Do you want to sit down?" I ask, showing him into the family room.

He sits in my father's chair, and I sit at one end of the couch. A hundred miles away. Like we're strangers.

Nate starts by saying, "I know I really blew it at prom. It was such a bad night. I'm not that kind of a guy. I want another chance to prove it."

"You want to take me to prom next year?"

"Well, that, too." He smiles. "I was actually thinking about something sooner."

I don't commit one way or the other. "I saw the play, Thursday."

"You came?"

I nod.

"Did you like it? Did you hear me totally flub my lines and everyone trying not to laugh?"

"No, you were great. I loved it."

He rubs his palms together. "And I heard y'all won Division Two. Congratulations."

"Thanks," I say. What else did Sally tell him?

"Ella, I can't tell if you've forgiven me for being an idiot, but I'm really sorry. I'm also sorry for blaming everything on my complicated family. I know it's not an excuse for everything I do."

"My family's complicated, too," I insist.

He laughs, then gets serious again. "And I talked to my sister about you. She might not be mature enough to admit it, but I think she feels bad about the way she's been acting toward you. Anyway, I hope you'll let me make it up to you."

"Okay," I say, standing. I'm not all that sure about Sally, but I'm not going to blame Nate for her behavior, either. He's too adorable to not give another chance.

He hesitates, then stands. "I guess that's my cue to go."

At the door I say, "Thank you for coming over," very formally.

But there's just one more thing.

On tiptoes I lean into him and put my no-longer-fat lips to his. I close my eyes, and feel his surprise and then his hands cupping my face gently. We stand there for nearly a minute, kissing. His lips are warm, and he tastes like candy. Light stubble rubs my cheeks, and I can barely breathe from the five million feelings I have bombarding me. If he weren't holding onto me, I might drift away like a balloon.

When I pull away, his eyes are still half closed. Then he opens

THROWING LIKE A GIRL

them slowly and says, "Ella Kessler, I've wanted to do that since the first time I saw you."

"Really?"

He smiles. Our faces are close. "Yes. And, if I don't go now, your father will catch us, and he'll never let me come back."

I wave as he jogs out to his car. He nearly trips, and I giggle. After he drives away I walk out to the yard, where my parents are surveying the garden, talking about what to do with a space by the garage, where they've removed some hedges.

They don't see me and I decide to stand here for a minute watching them. It's a perfect, sunny day, and as much as I love softball, I feel happy to have the season behind me. And next year's ahead of me. But before then, I have summer to look forward to and three friends to share it with.

Turns out, being fifteen's been pretty spectacular.